NOT A PE

The TARDIS, looking [...]
ioned London police telephone [...]
a pleasant suburban park. The Doctor and his young
journalist companion, Sarah Jane Smith, stepped out
into the bright sunlight.

"So where can we be?"

"Somewhere in London," said the Doctor.

"Are we in the future or the past?" Sarah persisted.

"We have probably returned to Earth at much
the same time we left."

An hour later, they had reached Shepherd's Bush,
an older and less suburban area of West London.
In all the miles they had walked, they hadn't seen
a sign of life anywhere. Halfway down the street of
little houses a large warehouse was set back from
the road. Its big double doors stood wide open. The
Doctor and Sarah ran down the street.

"Hello? Anyone at home?"

There was no response. Sarah was staring toward
a gloomy far corner of the warehouse. Something
was moving there.

"Doctor," she said, quietly, "I think there's someone over there."

The Doctor turned. "Hello?" he called. "We really
don't mean you any harm."

With a shriek the thing in the far corner floated
up into the air. Sarah couldn't believe what she was
now seeing—a pterodactyl, the flesh-eating flying
reptile that was once the master species on Earth.
Its leathery wings, eight feet wide, began to flap. Its
toothed mouth was wide open as it dived down
toward the Doctor and Sarah. . . .

(*please turn page*)

THE FOURTH DOCTOR WHO

This episode features the fourth Doctor Who, who has survived three reincarnations. The long trailing scarf, the floppy wide-brimmed hat, the mop of curly hair and the wide-eyed stare—all these are the obvious trademarks of the fourth Doctor Who. Along with a delightful mix of personality traits—genius and clown, hero and buffoon—the fourth Doctor Who combines the best of all who preceded him.

DOCTOR WHO'S COMPANIONS

SARAH JANE SMITH

Sarah is an independent freelance journalist. She has a mind of her own and once, while in search of a story, stowed away on Doctor Who's TARDIS—and ended up in the medieval past. Forever swearing she will never again set foot in the TARDIS, Sarah cannot resist the Doctor's plea that she accompany him one more time. While Sarah appears quite invulnerable, she really does need a bit of protection now and then.

THE BRIGADIER

Brigadier Alastair Lethbridge-Stewart is the Commanding Officer of the British branch of UNIT. UNIT, by the way, is the United Nations Intelligence Taskforce, created to protect the planet Earth from extraterrestrial invasion. The Brigadier is everyone's idea of the typical British Officer—his voice is clipped, his manner is abrupt, and his mustache is neat. But he is hardly robot-like. He's really very fond of the eccentric Doctor but sometimes he finds him very difficult to work with.

AND THE DINOSAUR INVASION
Malcolm Hulke

with an Introduction by
Harlan Ellison

22

PINNACLE BOOKS • NEW YORK

DOCTOR WHO AND THE DINOSAUR INVASION (#3)

A Pinnacle Books edition, published by special arrangement with W. H. Allen & Co., Ltd. First published in Great Britain by Universal-Tandem Publishing Co., Ltd. 1976.

First printing, May 1979
Second printing, May 1981
Third printing, February 1983

ISBN: 0-523-41613-X

Cover illustration by David Mann

Printed in the United States of America

PINNACLE BOOKS, INC.
1430 Broadway
New York, New York 10018

Introducing *DOCTOR WHO*

amenities performed by
HARLAN ELLISON

They could not have been more offended, confused, enraged and startled. . . . There was a moment of stunned silence . . . and then an eruption of angry voices from all over the fifteen-hundred-person audience. The kids in their Luke Skywalker pajamas (cobbled up from older brother's castoff karate *gi*) and the retarded adults spot-welded into their Darth Vader fright-masks howled with fury. But I stood my ground, there on the lecture platform at the World Science Fiction Convention, and I repeated the heretical words that had sent them into animal hysterics:

"*Star Wars* is adolescent nonsense; *Close Encounters* is obscurantist drivel; 'Star Trek' can turn your brains to purée of bat guano; and the greatest science fiction series of all time is *Doctor Who*! And I'll take you all on, one-by-one or all in a bunch to back it up!"

Auditorium monitors moved in, truncheons ready to club down anyone foolish enough to try jumping the lecture platform; and finally there was relative silence. And I heard scattered voices screaming from the back of the room, "Who?" And I said, "Yes. Who!"

(It was like that old Abbott and Costello routine: Who's on first? No, Who's on third; What's on first.)

After a while we got it all sorted out and they understood that when I said Who I didn't mean *whom*, I meant Who . . . Doctor Who . . . the most famous science fiction character on British television. The renegade Time Lord, the far traveler through Time and Space, the sword of justice from the planet Gallifrey, the scourge of villains and monsters the galaxy over.

The one and only, the incomparable, the bemusing and bewildering Doctor Who, the humanistic defender of Good and Truth whose exploits put to shame those of Kimball Kinnison, Captain Future and pantywaist nerds like Han Solo and Luke Skywalker.

My hero! Doctor Who!

For the American reading (and television-viewing) audience (and in this sole, isolated case I hope they're one and the same) *Doctor Who* is a new factor in the equation of fantastic literature. Since 1963 the Doctor and his exploits have been a consistent element of British culture. But we're only now being treated to the wonderful universes of Who here in the States. For those of us who were exposed to both the TV series on BBC and the long series of *Doctor Who* novels published in Great Britain, the time of solitary proselytizing is at an end. All we need to do now is thrust a Who novel into the hands of the unknowledgeable, or drag the unwary to a TV set and turn it on as the good Doctor goes through his paces. That's all it takes. Try this book and you'll understand.

I envy you your first exposure to this amazing conceit. And I wish for you the same delight I felt when Michael Moorcock, the finest fantasist in the English-speaking world, sat me down in front of his set in London, turned on the telly, and said, "Now be quiet and just watch."

That was in 1975. And I've been hooked on "Doctor Who" ever since. Understand: I despise television (having written it for sixteen years) and I spend much of my time urging people to bash in their picture tubes with Louisville Sluggers, to free themselves of the monster of the coaxial cable. And so, you must perceive that I speak of something utterly extraordinary and marvelous when I suggest you watch the "Doctor Who" series in whatever syndicated slot your local station has scheduled it. You must recognize that I risk all credibility for future exhortations by telling you *this* TV viewing will not harm you . . . will, in fact, delight and uplift you, stretch your imagination, tickle your risibilities, flinch your intellect of all lesser visual sf affections, improve your disposition and clean up your zits. What I'm saying here, case you're a *yotz* who needs things codified simply and directly, is that "Doctor Who" is the apex, the pinnacle, the tops, the Louvre Museum, the Coliseum, and other etcetera.

Now to give you a few basic facts about the Doctor, to brighten your path through this nifty series of lunatic novels.

He is a Time Lord: one of that immensely wise and powerful super-race of alien beings who, for centuries unnumbered, have watched and studied all of Time and Space with intellects (as H.G. Wells put it) vast and cool and unsympathetic. Their philosophy was never to interfere in the affairs of alien races, merely to watch and wait.

But one of their number, known only as the Doctor, found such inaction anathema. As he studied the interplay of great forces in the cosmos, the endless wars and invasions, the entropic conflict between Good and Evil, the rights and lives of a thousand alien life forms debased and brutalized, the wrongs left unrighted . . . he was overcome by the compulsion *to act*! He was a renegade, a misfit in the name of justice.

And so he stole a TARDIS and fled.

Ah, yes. The TARDIS. That most marvelous device for spanning the Time-lines and traversing all of known/unknown Space. The name is an acronym for Time And Relative Dimensions In Space. Marvelous! An amazing machine that can change shape to fit in with any locale in which it materializes. But the TARDIS stolen from his fellow Time Lords by the Doctor was in for repairs. And so it was frozen in the shape of its first appearance: a British police call box. Those of you who have been to England may have seen such call boxes. (There are very few of them extant currently, because the London "bobbies" now have two-way radio in their patrol cars; but before the advent of that communication system the tall, dark blue street call box—something like our old-fashioned wooden phone booth—was a familiar sight in the streets of London. If a police officer needed assistance he could call in directly from such a box, and if the station house wanted to get in touch with a copper they could turn on the big blue light atop the box and its flashing would attract a "bobby.")

Further wonder: the outward size of the TARDIS does not reveal its relative size *inside*. The size of a phone booth outwardly, it is enormous within, holding many sections filled with the Doctor's super-scientific equipment.

Unfortunately, the stolen TARDIS needed more repairs than just the fixing of its shape-changing capabilities. Its steering mechanism was also wonky, and so the Doctor could never be certain that the coordinates he set for time and place of materializing would be correct. He might set course for the planet Karn . . . and wind up in Victorian London. He might wish to relax at an intergalactic pleasure resort . . . and pop into existence in Antarctica. He might lay in a course for the deadly gold mines of Voga . . . and appear in Renaissance Italy.

It makes for a chancy existence, but the Doctor takes it all unflinchingly. As do his attractive female traveling companions, whose liaisons with the Doctor are never sufficiently explicated for those of us with a nasty, suspicious turn of mind.

The Doctor *looks* human and, apart from his quirky way of thinking, even *acts* human most of the time. But he is a Time Lord, not a mere mortal. He has two hearts, a stable body temperature of 60°, and—not to stun you too much—he's approximately 750 years old. Or at least he was that age when the first of the 43 *Doctor Who* novels was written. God (or Time Lords) only knows how old he is now!

Only slightly less popular than the good Doctor himself are his arch-foes and the distressing alien monsters he battles through the pages of these wild books and in phosphor-dot reality on your TV screens. They seem endless in their variety: the Vardans, the Oracle, Fendahl, the virus swarm of the Purpose, The Master, the Tong of the Black Scorpion, the evil brain of Morbius, the mysterious energy force known as the Mandragora

Helix, the android clone Kraals, the Zygons, the Cybermen, the Ice Warriors, the Autons, the spore beast called the Krynoid and—most deadly and menacing of them all—the robot threat of the Daleks.

Created by mad Davros, the great Kaled scientist, the pepper-pot-shaped Daleks made such an impression in England when they were first introduced into the series that they became a cultural artifact almost immediately. Movies have been made about them, toys have been manufactured of Daleks, coloring books, Dalek candies, soaps, slippers, Easter eggs and even special Dalek fireworks. They rival the Doctor for the attention of a fascinated audience and they have been brought back again and again during the fourteen years the series has perpetuated itself on BBC television; and their shiveringly pleasurable manifestations have not been confined just to England and America. Doctor Who and the Daleks have millions of rabid fans in over thirty countries around the world.

Like the three fictional characters *every* nation knows—Sherlock Holmes, Tarzan and Superman—Doctor Who seems to have a universal appeal.

Let me conclude this paean of praise with these thoughts: hating *Star Wars* and "Star Trek" is not a difficult chore for me. I recoil from that sophomoric species of creation that excuses its simplistic cliche structure and homage to the transitory (as does *Star Wars*) as violently as I do from that which sententiously purports to be deep and intellectual when it is, in fact, superficial self-conscious twaddle (as does "Star Trek"). This is not to say that I am an ivory tower intellect whose doubledome can only support Proust or Descartes. When I was a little kid, and was reading everything I could lay hands on, I read the classics with joy, but enjoyed equally those works I've come to think of as "elegant trash": the Edgar Rice Burroughs novels, The Shadow, Doc Savage, Conan, comic books and Uncle Wiggly. They taught me a great deal of what I know about courage and truth and ethics in the world.

To that list I add *Doctor Who*. His adventures are sunk to the hips in humanism, decency, solid adventure and simple good reading. They are not classics, make no mistake. They can never touch the illuminative level of Dickens or Mark Twain or Kafka. But they are solid entertainment based on an understanding of Good and Evil in the world. They say to us, "You, too, can be Doctor Who. You, like the good Doctor, can stand up for that which is bright and bold and true. You can shape the world, if you'll only go and try."

And they do it in the form of *all* great literature . . . the cracking good, well-plotted adventure yarn. They are direct lineal heirs to the adventures of Rider Haggard and Talbot Mundy, of H.G. Wells and Jules Verne, of Mary Shelley and Ray Bradbury. They are worth your time.

And if you give yourself up to the Doctor's winsome ways, he will take substance and reality in your imagination. For that reason, for the inestimable goodness and delight in every *Doctor Who* adventure, for the benefits he proffers, I lend my name and my urging to read and watch him.

I don't think you'll do less than thank me for shoving you down with this book in your hands, and telling you . . . here's Who. Meet the Doctor.

The pleasure is all mine. And all yours, kiddo.

HARLAN ELLISON
Los Angeles

CONTENTS

DOCTOR WHO
AND THE DINOSAUR
INVASION

The Dinosaurs

Three hundred and fifty million years ago, reptiles became the first animals to breed on land. Reptilian land life developed into many forms, the first true dinosaurs, not more than six inches long, appearing during the Triassic* period. By one hundred and fifty million years ago, some reptiles had developed into giants. One, the Diplodocus, measured eighty-four feet from head to tip of tail, and must have weighed thirty-five tons. During the Age of the Reptiles, many varieties of dinosaurs—all enormous in size—spread and multiplied over the Earth's surface.

Then, over a very short period in geological terms, the dinosaurs died out. Their remains have been found in every continent. Was it a sudden change in the Earth's temperature that killed them off? Was it disease? Or did the newer and more nimble life forms, the mammals, attack and kill them? Perhaps no one will ever know.

Certainly no one ever expected them to come back.

* Triassic—after the three-fold mountain system in Germany. The first mammals, and also flies and termites, appeared at that time.

1

London Alert!

Shughie McPherson woke up that morning with a pounding headache. For a full half hour he lay on his untidy bed and stared at a crack in the ceiling. He was thinking about the muddle which was his life. In his thirty-seven years he had had more jobs than he could remember. He was married once, but that hadn't lasted long. One day his wife had said to him, "Shughie, you're a layabout!" Then she'd packed a suitcase and gone back home to her mother. He had never tried to find her.

That was years ago. His mind turned to more recent events. About a week ago some of his Glasgow friends had said, "Shughie, we're going to London for the Cup Final. Why not come along?"

"I've nae money," he explained. "You'll ha' to do without me this time."

"We're going in wee Jamie's van," they replied. "It'll cost you nothing."

Eight of them got into the van, two in front and six sitting on crates of beer in the back. By the time they reached London nine hours later, Shughie had forgotten where they were going or why. He was drunk.

He remembered waking up in this house the next morning. Donald Ewing, a ship's riveter from Clydeside, was shaking his shoulders.

"Shughie, rouse yoursel! We're awa' back to Glasgee!"

Shughie's sleepy brain tried to make sense of the situation. "But we're in London, and we're going to see the Cup."

"Not now we're not," said Donald. He was already fully dressed. "Everyone's got to leave London. It's an emergency."

Jamie, the owner of the van, came to the door of the little bedroom and yelled. "Will you no come and get in the van. Donald? I'm leaving in five seconds!"

Donald protested. "There's wee Shughie here, still in bed."

Jamie looked down at Shughie. "If you don't get yourself into my van double quick, you can stay here and die! Come on, Donald, let's be off."

The two men tumbled out of the room. Shughie thought they'd both gone mad. He turned over and went back to sleep.

When he woke up later the house was completely silent. Pangs of hunger drove him out of bed. Standing on the landing, he called out: "Donald? Jamie? Ian?"

No answer. He went down the stairs into the hall and called again. Still no answer. He stumbled into a back room, and through there into the kitchen. Here he found a cupboard well stocked with tinned food. He ripped open a tin of corned beef and gorged the contents. Finding some matches, he turned one of the knobs on the stove to make himself a cup of tea. Nothing happened. He tried another knob. No gas. Nothing strange in that. Many times in his life the Gas Company had disconnected his gas supply because he hadn't paid the bills. He went to the sink for a glass of water. The tap spat out a few drops, and no more. Well, maybe that bill hadn't been paid either. He returned to the back room where he'd noticed a television set: it didn't

2

work. He tried the lights: no electricity. Daylight was beginning to fail. He searched the cupboards for candles: there was a bundle next to the dead electricity meter. He lit one, stuck it to a saucer, and left it in the back room; then lit another and carried it to see by as he investigated the rest of the house. No one had told him whose house it was, but in one room he found children's toys, so he presumed a family lived there. In a front room there was a double bed. All the drawers in the room were open. Clothes were strewn about on the floor as though people had packed hurriedly, leaving behind what they didn't want to carry.

In the front bedroom, partly hidden at the back of the wardrobe, Shughie found the six bottles of whisky that were to be his only companions for the next four days.

After half an hour staring at the crack in the ceiling and thinking about his life, Shughie McPherson got up. Now, after four days, he had become accustomed to living in this house on his own. He kept hoping that his friends would come back, and had completely forgotten why or how they went away.

He stretched and yawned, pulled on his trousers and shirt and went down the stairs to open another tin of food. Then he remembered that last night he'd eaten the last tin of corned beef and drunk the last drop of whisky. Standing in the hallway, he scratched his throbbing head, and decided the time had come for action.

He went to the house next door and knocked. The front door was unlocked. It swung open when he pushed it.

"Hello?" he called out.

No answer.

He stepped into the hall. "Anyone at home?"

3

Still no answer.

"I'm from the house next door. There's no food or water or anything . . ." He listened. Silence.

He tried the next house. The door was locked. He pressed the buzzer, but it didn't ring. "Probably didn't pay their electricity bill either," he said to himself, and moved on again. No answer this time, either. Shughie began to wish he was back in Glasgow, in the friendly district where he had always lived.

A sudden panic gripped him. Where were all the people who lived in these strange houses? Were they all dead?

He started running and shouting. Street after street was deserted, front doors of houses gaping open. And then turning a corner, he sighed with relief: a familiar sight. A friendly milk truck was standing in the middle of the road.

Shughie ran forward. "Hey! Milkman! Where are you?"

He stopped dead. The milkman was lying on the road on the other side of the float. He was a young man with very fair hair. He lay on his back, mouth open, eyes staring death.

Cautiously, very afraid, Shughie crept forward to look at the dead young milkman. The fair hair at the back of the young man's head was a tangle of congealed blood and gravel from the surface of the road.

Shughie fell to his knees, clasped his hands together, and started to say the Lord's Prayer. "Our Father who art in Heaven, hallow'd be thy name . . ."

His words were drowned by a sudden roar from the monster behind him. Shughie turned and looked up. A massive claw hit him in the face. In his last moment of life, Shughie McPherson resolved to give up drinking whisky.

4

The TARDIS, looking as always like an old-fashioned London police telephone box, materialized in a pleasant suburban park. The Doctor and his young journalist companion, Sarah Jane Smith, stepped out into bright sunlight.

Sarah looked about and sniffed a little dubiously. "It *seems* all right." She was hoping they hadn't landed in the poisonous atmosphere of some distant planet.

"Of course it's all right! I promised that I'd get you back home safely," replied the Doctor indignantly.

Sarah looked at some abandoned cricket stumps on the grass near by. "We set off from the research center, not here."

"Don't expect miracles," snapped the Doctor. "The coordinates were a bit off beam. But we can't be far away from UNIT Headquarters."

"So where can we be?"

"Somewhere in London," said the Doctor.

"And what about the date?" Sarah persisted. "Are we in the future or the past?"

"Time is relative." The Doctor locked the TARDIS and pocketed the key. "My guess is that we have returned to Earth at much the time we left. Now let's find a public telephone and inform the Brigadier that we're back."

The Doctor strode away toward some distant metal railings at the edge of the park. Sarah was about to follow, but paused when she heard a sound coming from the opposite direction. She turned and saw a clump of trees half a mile away. One of the trees came crashing to the ground. She caught up with the Doctor.

"What made that happen?"

He shrugged. "Some disease that trees get, I imagine. Now come on."

Five minutes later they reached the road that ran along the edge of the park.

5

Sarah said, "There's no traffic."

"Can't you imagine life without smelly motor cars?" The Doctor started to cross the road, Sarah following. He was hurrying toward a public telephone kiosk.

"It just seemed strange," she said.

"Nothing seems strange." said the Doctor, opening the door of the telephone kiosk, "when you've seen the places I have been to . . . " He stopped short. The telephone had been ripped from the wall, the coin box smashed open.

Sarah said, "It's been vandalized."

"I wish people wouldn't use that term," said the Doctor. "The Vandals were quite decent chaps."

"I suppose you've met them?" Sarah asked, tongue-in-cheek.

"As a matter of fact, yes. We'll have to find a taxi." The Doctor turned from the telephone kiosk and regarded the deserted road.

"How," asked Sarah, "do we find a taxi when there is no traffic?"

"Perhaps it's a Sunday," said the Doctor. "Great Britain always closes on Sundays. We'll have to walk."

Twenty minutes later they reached a suburban shopping center. Sarah pointed across the street excitedly.

"Look," she said, keeping up with the Doctor, "Woolworth's!"

"What is so special about Woolworth's?"

"Nothing," said Sarah, "but it's nice to see. It means we're back home."

The Doctor paused. "Really, Sarah! I take you in the TARDIS to Outer Space, to another Time in the history of the Universe, and what really excites you?— *Woolsworth's!*"

His words were drowned by the roar of a car speeding along the high street. It was the first sign of life they'd seen since their return to Earth. Sarah stepped out into the road, waving her arms, smiling.

"Hey! Stop!"

The car kept going. Moving fast, the Doctor grabbed Sarah back to safety.

"He almost hit me!" she gasped.

"Perhaps he doesn't like hitchhikers."

They watched the car race down the street. At an intersection with dead traffic lights the driver swung the car to the crown of the road, then turned left with a screech of brakes.

"Have you noticed there aren't even any parked cars?" Sarah said.

"I agree," said the Doctor. "It is a bit odd. Let's keep walking. There must be someone somewhere."

They continued toward the traffic lights. Sarah stopped and pointed. "Look! That car! It's stopped."

The car was standing outside a jeweler's shop. Without a word, the Doctor and Sarah ran toward it. The car's engine was running, but there was no driver.

"The driver must have gone inside," Sarah said, entering the open shop door.

"Don't be hasty," called the Doctor. But it was already too late. Sarah had gone into the shop. The Doctor followed.

Sarah was standing in the middle of the shop looking in wonder at the cases of expensive rings, necklaces, and the displays of wrist watches.

"Look at all these lovely things," she gasped, "and the door wide open."

"The door has been forced open," said the Doctor. "Now come on, let's go."

The Doctor turned, and found himself looking into the twin spouts of a sawed-off shotgun. Holding the gun was the driver of the car, a young man with greasy black hair and badly bitten fingernails.

7

"I got here first," said the man. "Turn around and, put your hands against the wall."

Sarah protested, "You nearly ran me down!"

The man waved the gun at her. "I said put your hands against the wall!"

The Doctor turned and spread out his hands on the wall. "Do as he says, Sarah."

Sarah put her hands against the wall, her back to the man. Looking under her arm, she could see him scooping precious rings and necklaces into a leather bag.

"I appreciate that you're very busy," said the Doctor calmly, "but could you tell us what's going on?"

"You find your own places," said the man. "There's plenty to choose from."

"We don't want to find any *places*," the Doctor answered. "We just want to know why the streets are deserted."

"Because they are," said the man. His bag was now brimming with valuables. "If you both stay exactly where you are, I won't hurt you." He laughed. "In any case, I'm leaving you plenty of stuff here!"

He dashed out of the shop. Sarah immediately made for the door. The Doctor checked her.

"No, Sarah! He may shoot you in panic!"

They listened as the car sped away. Sarah hurried across the ransacked shop to a telephone on a ledge behind the counter. She scooped it up and dialled 999.

"There's no ringing tone. Nothing. It's dead."

"The sooner we reach the Brigadier, the better," the Doctor replied.

"But do you realize we've got no idea where we are?"

"That's easily fixed." The Doctor went behind one of the counters and quickly found the shop's account books and stationery. He read from an invoice, "THE LITTLE SHOP, ACTION. So we're in West London. All we have to do is strike east."

8

"It'll be a long walk."

"Don't forget you're over seven hundred years younger than me, so you should be able to manage it. Let's make a start."

They came out of the shop. Sarah looked up and down the deserted street. "Which way is east?"

The Doctor produced a small compass from the capacious pockets of his coat, and held it steady until the needle stopped rotating. "That way." He pointed up the high street.

After a few steps Sarah paused. "Doctor, I'm really very hungry."

"If you'd mentioned that while we were still in the TARDIS, I could have fixed you a meal in no time."

"Those pills from the machine?" She pulled a face. "I'd like something *real* to eat."

"There's plenty to choose from here." He pointed out some of the signs in the street. "CHINESE TAKE AWAY, WIMPY'S, BERT'S CAFE. Take your pick."

The door to Bert's Cafe was standing open. Sarah crossed the empty street, followed by the Doctor.

The little cafe had plastic-top tables, a counter on one side by the door, and a sign that read THANKS FOR YOUR CUSTOM. PLEASE CALL AGAIN. BERT. Sarah saw a large ham on the counter. Her mouth watered and she went straight to the ham—then recoiled when she saw the flies clustered on it. "The food's gone rotten."

But the Doctor was concentrating on the partly eaten plates of food on some of the tables. "Just like the *Marie Celeste*," he muttered.

"The what?"

"A very famous incident in the last century," he explained. "A ship called the *Marie Celeste* was found on the high seas, intact but totally abandoned. The crew and all the passengers had vanished as though they never existed. And, just as here, partly eaten meals

9

were left on plates in the dining room. No one ever discovered what happened to the people on that ship, and they never will."

A cold shiver of fear ran down Sarah's spine. "Suddenly I don't feel hungry," she said.

The Doctor smiled. "Don't worry, Sarah. There must be some logical explanation for all this. Take a couple of bars of chocolate from that shelf. I'm sure you'll be able to eat them later. And, as you said, we've got a long walk ahead of us."

Sarah picked up the chocolate, and placed a few pennies on top of the till. "The people eating in here must have all left in a hurry. But why?"

"Why. indeed?" replied the Doctor. "Now let's recommence our long walk."

An hour later they had reached Shepherd's Bush, an older and less suburban area of West London. In all the miles they had walked they hadn't seen a sign of life anywhere. Sarah stopped.

"I'm whacked."

The Doctor looked about the street they were walking down. "Let's try the Times Furnishing Company over there." He pointed and grinned. "The shop door's open. Surely we'll find a seat in there."

"There's no need to be funny," she said. "Come on, we'll press ahead."

As they started off again they both heard the sound of the truck. Without a word they stopped, listening intently.

Sarah said, "Where is it?"

The Doctor put his finger to his lips. "Shhh!"

The sound of the lorry altered as its driver changed into reverse gear.

"That street over there," said the Doctor, pointing to a side street, "and it's backing up for some reason."

They hurriedly crossed the main road to the opening of the side street from where they could hear the truck. As they entered the side street, the sound of the truck's engine stopped.

"We've lost it," said Sarah.

"I don't think so," said the Doctor. "Look down there."

Half way down the street of little houses a large warehouse was set well back from the road. Big double doors stood wide open and the nose of a truck protruded out onto a tarmac apron. The Doctor and Sarah ran down the street toward the truck. Sarah had forgotten all about her tiredness. As they approached the open double doors the Doctor started calling.

"Hello? Anyone at home?"

There was no response. The Doctor put his hand on the hood of the truck. "This must be the one we heard," he said. "It's warm. The engine has just been running."

Cautiously they edged along the side of the truck into the warehouse. It was filled with racks of expensive fur coats.

"With London deserted, why should anyone want to make a delivery of fur coats?" Sarah sounded puzzled.

The Doctor looked at an untidy heap of fur coats in the open back of the lorry. "I don't think they were making a delivery," he said, "but more a collection. I mean they were stealing these furs."

Suddenly two men, one gripping a vicious-looking jimmy, leapt out from behind one of the fur racks. Sarah screamed. The jimmy cracked down on the Doctor's mop of curly hair. Gripping his head in agony, he fell to the ground. The two men ran down by the side of the truck and escaped into the street. As Sarah knelt down by the Doctor, he opened his eyes and put his hand to his head.

"That's going to be a nasty bump," he said. With Sarah's help he struggled to his feet, a little unsteadily. "At least they've provided us with some transport. Let's see if they left the ignition key."

The Doctor started to edge down the side of the truck toward the cabin. But Sarah was staring toward a gloomy far corner of the warehouse. Something was moving there.

"Doctor," she said, quietly, "I think there's someone over there."

The Doctor turned. "Hello?" he called. "If you're another fur thief, we really don't mean you any harm. All *we* want to take is the lorry. The furs you can keep."

With a shriek the thing in the far corner floated up into the air. Sarah couldn't believe what she was now seeing—a pterodactyl, the flesh-eating flying reptile that was once the master species on Earth. Its leathery wings, eight feet wide, flapped and its toothed mouth was wide open as it dived down toward the Doctor and Sarah.

"Get in the cabin," shouted the Doctor.

Sarah struggled into the truck's cab and hastily slammed the door behind her. Outside, the Doctor grabbed one of the furs and flapped it at the attacking pterodactyl. The flying reptile pulled back and hovered for some moments before attacking again. But the pause gave the Doctor the vital seconds he needed to get into the cabin and behind the driving wheel. The ignition key was in the fascia board and he turned it. The self-starter worked, but the engine didn't fire. As the Doctor tried again, the pterodactyl landed on the roof of the cab and leaned over to look at his prey through the windscreen. On the third try, the engine sprang into life. The Doctor slipped the truck into gear and roared out of the warehouse into the street. Through the rear mirror he saw the pterodactyl turn and fly off in the opposite direction.

Sarah, petrified, stared straight ahead. "I can't believe it. I simply can't believe it. Those things died out millions of years ago."

"During the Earth's Cretaceous period to be exact," shouted the Doctor above the noise of the truck, as he turned it into the main road and again headed east. "Next to the tyrannosaurus rex, they must have been the most terrifying creatures this planet has ever produced."

"Honestly," said Sarah, exasperated, "that's just typical! We're attacked by a monster, and you talk about it like a schoolmaster! That thing could have killed us. And what's it doing here in London in the Twentieth Century?"

"That," said the Doctor, "is something we may soon find out. Look what's ahead."

An Army jeep was blocking the road. Two soldiers with guns, and a sergeant with a bullhorn, were standing by it, facing the oncoming truck. The Doctor drew up close to the jeep, jumped out of the cab and walked toward the sergeant.

"My dear fellow," said the Doctor, smiling, "I'm so glad to meet you—"

The sergeant raised the bullhorn to his lips and spoke into its microphone. His voice was harsh. "Stay where you are! If you advance any further you will be shot!"

The Doctor stopped dead in amazement. "But I just wanted to ask you—"

The voice from the bullhorn drowned the Doctor's words. "The person in the cab of the truck is to dismount immediately, or we shall fire!"

The Doctor turned to Sarah. "You'd better do as he says."

Nervously, Sarah climbed down from the cab.

"Neither of you is to budge an inch," continued the amplified voice of the sergeant. Dropping the bullhorn,

13

he turned to the two soldiers. "Smith, keep them covered—and shoot to maim if they move. Wilkins, hop around the back and see what they've got."

The soldier called Wilkins ran to the back of the truck while the Doctor and Sarah waited.

"If you will let me explain," said the Doctor, "I and my young friend—"

The bullhorn cut in. "Be quiet!" The sergeant turned to the soldier called Smith. "Hold that gun steady."

Smith aimed his gun directly at the Doctor's head, finger on trigger. Wilkins returned from the back of the truck carrying one of the fur coats.

"They've got a load of furs in the back like this one, sarge. There must be thousands of dollars' worth!"

The sergeant again raised the bullhorn to his lips. Speaking through it gave him great authority. "I'm placing both of you under arrest. You know what happens to looters. Now it's going to happen to you."

2

Shoot To Kill!

"With great respect, sir," said Brigadier Lethbridge-Stewart, "I cannot and will not order troops under my command to open fire on civilians!"

"These civilians are looters," said General Finch, "the lowest form of life known to man. You will tell your troops to shoot to kill!"

The General and the Brigadier stood facing each other in UNIT's temporary Headquarters—a school classroom in North London, on the edge of the area that had been evacuated. A huge map of London, with flags to indicate where pterodactyls and dinosaurs had been sighted, had been pinned over the blackboard. A military two-way radio, manned constantly by a UNIT soldier, had been installed in a corner.

The Brigadier tried to control the emotion in his voice. "I cannot, sir, order the murder of people who may be innocent."

The General's face reddened. His closely cropped moustache twitched. "Every man, woman and child in the Central London area has been evacuated by order of the Government. It has become a prohibited area. It follows, therefore, that any civilian now found in Central London is up to no good—and that means they are using this opportunity to rob and steal. There is only one thing to do—to shoot on sight!"

"I agree that what is happening is deplorable, sir,"

15

said the Brigadier, "but may I remind you that looters are *not* our main problem, and shortage of observation patrols *is*. Can't more troops be brought to London?"

"Definitely not. They're needed in the reception areas. You're forgetting that ten million people have to be fed, sheltered, and cared for. That's what the Army is doing, Brigadier. Helping all those poor people who have been driven from their city."

"I realize that," continued the Brigadier, "but the front line is *here*. I think it's more important that we find the cause of the crisis than try to deal with its effects."

The General rocked on his heels, clutching his swagger cane behind his back. "On that I agree with you, Brigadier. May I ask what you're doing about it?"

The Brigadier explained that his UNIT troops were fully occupied in plotting the sightings of monsters.

"And do you call that *doing* something?" smirked the General. "Where is this famous scientific adviser of yours?"

"Temporarily on leave, sir." It was a white lie. He had no idea where the Doctor was at this moment.

"Really?" said the General. "How inconvenient. Should he decide to return, do you think he may be able to help us with our problem?"

"In all honesty, sir, if anyone can find out why dinosaurs keep appearing and disappearing all over London, it's the Doctor."

"Then the sooner you recall him from leave, Brigadier, the better." The General turned to go, then paused. "I shall let you have some extra men, seconded to UNIT from the British Army. But their orders will be to shoot to kill! I hope you understand that."

The General marched out of the classroom. The Brigadier sighed with relief, and slumped into the chair behind his makeshift desk. He turned to Sergeant Benton, who had remained standing to attention throughout the General's visit.

"Sergeant, you've no idea where the Doctor is, have you?"

"He could be anywhere, sir," said Benton. "But I wish he was here to help us."

The Doctor and Sarah were standing between armed soldiers in a drafty church hall. Ahead of them another prisoner, a tough-looking young man in a dirty raincoat, was being questioned by an Army sergeant seated at a bench desk.

"Name?"

"Lodge."

The sergeant wrote down "Lodge" on the top of a blank sheet of typewriting paper. "Age?"

"Twenty-two."

The sergeant noted the prisoner's age, then turned to the armed soldier standing beside Lodge. "What had he got?"

The soldier reeled off a list of goods found in the possession of the prisoner. "Two tape recorders, one radio, and a color television set."

"Right, my lad," said the sergeant to Lodge, "you know where you're going. Take him away!"

The soldier yanked on Lodge's arm and steered him to a far corner of the big hall. The soldiers guarding the Doctor and Sarah pushed them roughly toward the sergeant's desk. The sergeant placed a fresh sheet of paper before him.

"Names?" He didn't look up when he asked the question.

"If I could have a word with someone in authority—" the Doctor blurted out.

The soldier standing behind the Doctor shouted in his ear, "Quiet! Answer the Sergeant's question!"

17

"Names?" The sergeant repeated his question, still not looking up. He had been on duty for many hours without sleep. He was tired. He hated looters.

Sarah spoke up. "Sarah Jane Smith." Then she added quickly, "But you've got to listen to us, please. I'm a journalist. This is all a big mistake!"

The sergeant wrote down Sarah's name, and then looked up at the Doctor, ignoring Sarah completely. "And your name?"

"Dr. John Smith," said the Doctor, realizing that the sergeant would never believe he hadn't really got a name. He remembered to add, "We're not related."

The sergeant wrote "Dr. John Smith." Then he asked, "Ages? The girl first."

Sarah said, "Twenty-three."

"You'd never believe me if I told you," the Doctor replied.

The sergeant shrugged. "It doesn't really matter. Age is no excuse for what you people have done." He turned to the soldier standing behind the Doctor. "What had they got?"

"The patrol said they'd got furs in the back of a truck."

The sergeant wrote down "furs." Then he looked up. "Right. You'll be held for military trial."

"Just one question," said Sarah. "Why are the military running everything? Where are the police?"

The sergeant pushed his chair back, stretched his arms and yawned. His eyes were bloodshot with tiredness. "You were found in the Central Zone, which you know is under martial law. Only the military are allowed in the Central Zone."

"But why?" asked the Doctor earnestly. "What's happening?"

The sergeant looked at the soldiers guarding the two prisoners. "You've got a right couple of nutters here."

18

He turned back to the Doctor. "Don't you ever read the newspapers, or listen to the news on the radio?"

"We've been rather a long way away," expalined the Doctor.

"Come off it! There's nowhere in the world doesn't know about what's happening here," said the sergeant, clearly bored by the Doctor's presence. "All right, lads, take 'em away for their mug shots."

The soldier pushed the Doctor and Sarah to one corner of the church hall where an Army photographer was waiting. They were told to stand facing the camera while a soldier held across their chests their prisoner numbers. Then they were both photographed in profile.

Sarah asked the soldiers, "Do you get pleasure out of treating us as common criminals?"

"We're treating you for what you are," said the soldier photographer. "If you hadn't broken martial law you wouldn't be here." He took the final photograph. "All right, I've finished with them."

The soldiers pushed the couple toward the corner where Lodge was already sitting on the floor. One of the soldiers ordered them to sit on the floor.

"I'd rather stand, thank you," replied the Doctor.

The soldier leveled his gun at the Doctor. "I said sit down!"

The Doctor sat.

"What do we do now?" asked Sarah.

"Wait till an officer turns up." The Doctor inched over to where the young man Lodge was sitting, hunched up, chin between his knees. "How do you do!"

Lodge gave the Doctor a surly look. "You've got nothing to be cheerful about, mate."

The Doctor smiled. "Surely, this is only a misunderstanding."

"That's one way to look at it," said Lodge. "There's no judge, no jury. It's martial law."

Sarah shuffled over to Lodge. "But can you tell us why?"

"The monsters, of course. But you know about that already."

Sarah and the Doctor exchanged glances. The Doctor spoke to Lodge very patiently. "Let's pretend that my young companion and I have been for a trip into Outer Space, that we've only just returned, and we know nothing about these monsters. Now you tell us what happened."

Lodge grinned. "Outer Space? You must be joking."

"It's only a game," said Sarah. "You see, I'm a journalist. I want you to tell me what happened, from your point of view."

This approach made more sense to Lodge. He thought for a few seconds, then spoke. "It was about two weeks ago that they saw the first one—"

"Who?" said the Doctor, interrupting. "Where?"

"Some kids, I think, on Hampstead Heath. They went home and told their mom they'd seen a dinosaur. Naturally she didn't believe them. They found some friends of theirs, other kids, to go and have a look at it. Their bodies were found a few hours later."

Sarah closed her eyes in horror. "How terrible."

"Do go on," said the Doctor quietly.

"Later that day some sort of big bird was seen flying over Hyde Park. A lot of people saw it. But it wasn't a bird—not really. It was a . . . a . . . I can't remember the name for it."

"Pterodactyl?" said the Doctor.

"That's right! I've seen one of them—horrible-looking things. They've got no feathers, sort of naked. Anyway, that night a ruddy great big thing turned up in the car park by the Festival Hall. It tramped about, swinging its tail, and wrecked two hundred cars. The next day they were turning up everywhere, killing,

20

crushing motor cars, even walking straight through people's houses. There was hundreds of people killed."

Sarah asked, "But where had they come from?"

"Hold it a moment," the Doctor told her. "We'll talk about that later." He turned to Lodge. "What happened then?"

"It was panic, wasn't it? Everyone with a car packed everything they could get into it and drove out into the country. The Government declared martial law in London, and said everyone had to leave. They got trains and buses for them, and sent them all over the place."

"But where to?" asked Sarah.

Lodge shrugged. "They put 'em in peoples' houses in the country, I think. And they set up big camps for them. There's about ten million people gone, you know."

"What about yourself?" asked the Doctor.

Lodge grinned mischievously. "I stayed back for the pickings, didn't I? Same as you two." He looked over his shoulder at the soldier who was guarding them. "There's only him," he whispered. "We could make a break for it. Want to try?"

"I don't think so," said the Doctor. "We haven't done anything wrong. What I really want is to speak to someone in authority—"

A sergeant marched into the hall, banged his feet on the bare floorboards as he stood to attention, and shouted, "Right! On your feet!"

The soldier guarding them came over. "You heard the Sergeant! Jump to it!"

They stood up. A young Army lieutenant entered the hall, looked at the prisoners, then sat down at the desk. He took off his cap, placed it carefully on the desk, and spoke to the sergeant. "Bring them over, please."

The prisoners were herded toward the desk. "I'm terribly glad to meet you," said the Doctor, offering his hand. "This is just the opportunity I've been looking for to—"

The sergeant barked, "The prisoners will remain silent unless spoken to!"

The lieutenant asked, "What are the charges?"

The sergeant pointed to Lodge. "This one, sir, was found illegally in the Central Zone, and illegally in the possession of two tape recorders, one radio, and a color television set."

"Anything to say?" The lietuenant seemed very bored, and not at all interested in whatever the prisoner might have to say.

Lodge said, "I found the stuff, see. I was going to hand it in."

"Yes, I see," said the lieutenant, as though he had heard that story many times before. "You have been found guilty of looting. Under the authority vested in me by the Emergency Powers Act I am sending you to be held in detention for an indefinite period. You will be handed over to the civil authorities for trial and sentence when time permits. Next prisoner step forward."

The Doctor went up to the desk. "Lieutenant, I really must protest. My young companion and I are totally innocent of the charge—"

"Be quiet," said the lieutenant. "What *is* the charge?"

"Picked up with the girl," said the sergeant. "Found in possession of furs and a stolen truck."

"Anything to say?" asked the lieutenant.

"A great deal," said Sarah. "We found other people stealing those furs—"

"And you were going to hand them in?" queried the lieutenant, with an unconcealed sneer.

The question threw Sarah off her guard. "Not exactly," she admitted. "We were mainly concerned with escaping from a pterodactyl."

"And *I* think you were mainly concerned with getting

22

away with those furs," said the lieutenant. He cleared his throat before pronouncing verdict. "You are both found guilty of looting. Under the authority vested in me by the Emergency Powers Act I am empowered to hold you in detention for an indefinite period. You will be handed over to the civil authorities for trial and sentenced when time permits." He stood up and clapped on his cap. "Thank you, sergeant. Get them away from here as soon as possible."

"Yes, sir!" The sergeant stood to attention and saluted as the lieutenant hurried out of the church hall. The sergeant turned to the prisoners. "Back in your corners, you lot."

"I'm hungry," said Sarah. "Is starvation part of the punishment?"

"If you behave yourself, I'll get some food sent in to you." The sergeant turned and left the hall.

One soldier now remained to guard the prisoners. He leveled his gun at them. "Back to the corner, and sit down. You won't have long to wait. Transport will be arriving to take you to the detention center any minute now."

Seated on the floor once more, the Doctor turned to Lodge, "Did you say something about making a break for it, old man?"

"Doctor," exclaimed Sarah, quite shocked, "we mustn't do anything of the sort! We'll get ourselves into even more trouble."

"I hardly think that's possible," said the Doctor. "No one will listen to us. Escape seems the only way out of this mess." He turned back to Lodge. "How do you propose we get away?"

Lodge glanced round furtively at their guard. The soldier had sat down, his back to them. "There's three of us. We could jump him."

"My dear chap," said the Doctor, "let us be a little more subtle than that."

Lodge, whose friends didn't normally use such words as "subtle," turned to Sarah in despair. "What's the old geezer talking about?"

"The 'old geezer,'" she said, hotly, "is much brighter than you are, so listen to him!"

Lodge turned back to the Doctor. "All right. What's the plan?"

"We have a fight," said the Doctor.

Lodge didn't understand. "Eh?"

The Doctor put on a loud, Cockney accent. "It was you what grassed on us!"

Lodge understood now. In his world, "to grass" meant to give information to the police—the worst possible social behavior. He immediately reacted: "I never grassed in my life!"

The Doctor stood up, towering over Lodge. "Get on your feet, you low-down dirty stool pigeon!" "Stool pigeon" was another term that meant an informer.

Lodge jumped up and faced him. "You don't call me names like that and get away with it!"

"Don't I?" sneered the Doctor. "I know what they say about you in these parts. You've always been a copper's nark. Your family are well known for it."

This stung Lodge. The only loyalty he knew was to his immediate family. The insult deeply offended him. "All right, you great dressed-up twit," he bellowed. "You asked for it!" He swung his fist at the Doctor's face. The Doctor sidestepped, and landed a light blow to Lodge's chest.

Sarah screamed at the soldier: "Stop them!"

The soldier ran forward, waving his rifle as though he was about to strike his two struggling prisoners. Sarah stuck her foot out. The soldier tripped, tumbling forward. Lodge grabbed and held on to the rifle. The

24

Doctor caught the soldier, applying a Venusian karate hold to the man's neck. The soldier passed out, unconscious. The Doctor gently lowered him to the bare floorboards. Lodge watched in amazement.

"What did you do?"

"Never mind," said the Doctor. He looked around for means of escape. "We can get through that window." There was a brick wall opposite the window: clearly it let onto an alleyway.

Lodge aimed the gun at the Doctor. "You go through the door, the way we came in!"

"But we'll all three go together," Sarah said.

"Not while I've got the gun," said Lodge viciously. "You two—out through the door. While you're being overpowered by the soldiers, I'll go through the window."

Sarah stood up and faced Lodge. "You dirty cheat! We shouldn't have had anything to do with you."

Lodge grinned. "That's right. But then I didn't have your nice education, did I? Where I was brought up life was rough. You had to look after yourself or go under . . ." His attention focused on Sarah, he didn't notice the Doctor's quick move to come behind him. The Doctor's hands slipped round Lodge's neck, again applying the Venusian karate hold. Lodge gurgled for a moment, dropped the gun, then fell to the ground unconscious.

They raced to the window, climbed out into the alleyway. "This way," said the Doctor, grabbing Sarah's hand and dragging her toward the street that ran in front of the drill hall. As they came out into the street, the Doctor stopped. "Just what we need," he said, eyeing a parked Army truck. It was a small vehicle with a covered-in back. "In that we're not so likely to be stopped by military patrols."

The Doctor jumped into the driver's seat; Sarah got in beside him. He looked at the ignition switch.

"We're not in luck this time," Sarah said. "There's no key."

"But with a piece of wire I could jump the ignition. Let's see what they've got in the back."

The Doctor turned and slid back the door that led into the rear of the van, and looked straight into the snout of a leveled rifle.

"Ready to go to the detention center now?" asked the soldier. "Because this is the van that's going to take you!"

The Doctor and Sarah sat side by side in the back of the detention center van as it sped through the deserted streets of London. Their wrists were handcuffed together.

"Honestly, Doctor, that wasn't very clever," said Sarah reproachfully.

"How was I to know it was the detention center van?"

The van turned sharply, throwing them sideways. Sarah regained her crouched position on the hard wooden bench. "What do we do now?"

"Someone at the center will listen to us."

"No they won't," she said. "No one's listened to us up to now. I can see us being prisoners for months, probably sewing mail bags or whatever they have to do, and mixing with criminals . . ."

The van screamed to a stop, hurling them both forward. Suddenly, a thunderous roar made the van vibrate. The Doctor edged forward and slid open the door behind the driver's cab. The soldier-driver and his companion were scrambling out, guns in hand. Through the windscreen the Doctor could see the gigantic shape of a tyrannosaurus rex blocking the road.

26

"What is it?" Sarah shouted.

"Come over here," said the Doctor, sliding the door back a few more inches. "That's one of the biggest and deadliest land animals that has ever existed on your planet."

Sarah looked and gasped. The tyrannosaurus rex was standing upright on its two hind legs, balancing on an enormous tail. Head raised, it was considerably taller than a double-decker bus. Compared with its huge head and six-inch-long teeth, its little two-fingered "hands" looked weak and futile. The two soldiers were crouched against the buildings on either side of the street, firing their automatic guns into the reptile's neck. The monster roared with pain and anger as dribbles of bright red blood flowed down its leathery green skin.

"I've always wanted to study one of those," said the Doctor, observing the scene in his typically scientific manner.

"Well I haven't!" screamed Sarah.

"During their heyday," the Doctor went on, as though oblivious to the danger they were in, "they dominated all other living creatures except the pterodactyls, which could fly away. Do you notice the way the serrated teeth curve backward?"

"I've got my eyes closed," Sarah replied, honestly.

"That was to tear at their victims. Another thing about the tyrannosaurus rex," he continued, "was that they were much more intelligent than all the other giant reptiles. That still meant they were pretty stupid compared with the smallest mammal. But it gave them a great advantage."

"Doctor, do you think we could have the natural history lesson some other time? I'm terrified!"

"Of course, my dear," he said. "How inconsiderate of me. With our soldier guards so preoccupied, this is an excellent opportunity to escape. Come along."

He grabbed her by the hand so that the handcuffs wouldn't tug at their wrists, and went through the doorway into the driver's cab. The soldier-driver had cautiously removed the ignition key before jumping out to fight the monster.

"We'll have to run for it," said the Doctor, helping Sarah down on to the road. "I suggest we go *away* from our reptile friend."

"What a brilliant idea. I'd never have thought of it."

The Doctor didn't react to her sarcasm. He started running, Sarah beside him. As they neared the end of the street there was an explosion behind them. They stopped and turned. A cloud of smoke filled the street near the reptile's tail. One of the soldiers threw another hand-grenade at the reptile. It exploded with a brilliant flash and a *boom* that must have been heard miles away.

"That," said the Doctor, "should bring every soldier in this part of London to this street. The sooner we find somewhere to hide, the better."

They hurried on down the next street. Then the Doctor stopped abruptly.

"A mews," he said.

"A what?" asked Sarah.

The Doctor pointed to a small opening off the street they were now in. The opening led to a cobblestone mews, a narrow street lined with garages.

"In days gone by," said the Doctor, "London's mews were for the stables of the gentry. Now they have all been turned into garages. Garages have work benches, vices, and files. Let's see what we can find."

As the Doctor had predicted, the entire mews was lined with big garage doors, most of them carrying the words IN CONSTANT USE—NO PARKING. There wasn't a car in sight.

"Won't they all be locked?" Sarah asked.

The Doctor moved from door to door, testing them. "Under the circumstances," he said, "hardly likely. Remember all the shop doors we found open? Ah!" He had found a little door let into the bigger doors of the garage—and it was unlocked! "Mind the step," he warned, and went through into the garage, tugging Sarah after him. Inside, a little daylight filtered through a filthy window at the far end. The floor of the garage was thick with black oil. There were various machines for car repairs, and a well-equipped work bench. Clamped to the work bench was a vice.

"Exactly what we need," said the Doctor. "Now all we want is a file." He looked along the tool shelf, found a foot-long file. "Let's get your cuff open first."

Sarah held her wrist so that part of the metal cuff encircling it was between the plates of the vice. The Doctor screwed up the vice, closing the plates in onto the metal cuff. Then he started to file through it.

"Where did that monster come from?" Sarah asked.

"The Upper Cretaceous Period."

"I mean how did it come to be here in London today?" she persisted.

"Ah," he said, "a very good question."

"Don't you know the answer?"

"That isn't such a good question," he said, working hard with the file. "How could I possibly know?" He paused. "Am I hurting you?"

"Not yet," she said. She could see that she might be hurt once the file neared her flesh.

He continued filing. "Since the only people we have spoken to up to now have been either criminals or rather stupid soldiers, I haven't much to go on."

Sarah tried to work it out. "Suppose there was an egg buried in the ground somewhere, and somehow or other it hatched!"

29

"Producing a sweet little baby monster?" asked the Doctor, smiling.

"Yes," she said, enthusiastically. Then she realized the fallacy in that idea. "But how did it grow to that size without anyone noticing?"

"Maybe someone kept it as a pet," said the Doctor, "and turned it out when it got too big to feed."

"You're making fun of me."

"Because I think you've forgetting the pterodactyl. I'm almost through now. Grit your teeth in case I hurt you."

Sarah closed her eyes and nerved herself to feel the file run across the flesh of her wrist. But the Doctor took great care. After a moment Sarah felt the cuff fall away from her wrist. She opened her eyes.

"Thanks." She rubbed her wrist.

Wasting no time, the Doctor opened the vice a fraction of an inch, let the remains of Sarah's cuff fall to the floor, then put his own cuff in the vice and set to work again with the file.

"You see," he said, "we are talking about many reptiles, not just one. According to that unpleasant young man we met in the drill hall, there have been a large number of monsters popping up."

"Could it be something that we're all imagining?" asked Sarah hopefully. "A kind of mass hallucination?"

"It's possible—but unlikely. You can, if you know how, hypnotize a whole crowd of people, and make them believe they're seeing all sorts of things. But I don't think you could do it to millions of people spread all over a city the size of London."

"Then what is the explanation?"

"I think it's got something to do with Time," speculated the Doctor. "There! I'm through!" He opened the vice, and the cuff fell to the floor. "People tend to think of Time as being inflexible, with a beginning, a middle,

30

and an end. But if you apply Einstein's Theory of Relativity to the question of Time, you find that it *may* move in great curves . . ."

His voice trailed off. He was staring toward a darkened corner of the garage.

Sarah said, "What is it?"

"I think we are not alone," he said. He raised his voice. "Hello, old chap. What can we do for you?"

Sarah watched, her heart beating fast, as a man came forward from the corner. He was about forty with long straggly hair and a faded blue smock that came down to his knees. On his feet were crudely made leather shoes, encrusted with mud. His right hand clutched a rusted knife.

"Back, back, accursed wizard!" He spoke with a strong Midlands accent.

"We're not wizards," replied the Doctor quietly. "There's nothing to be afraid of. Do you know where you are?"

The man's frightened eyes darted from the Doctor to Sarah.

"The witch," he said. "She put a spell on me. I shall tell the priest and he will burn her at the stake."

"Do you know what year it is?" asked the Doctor.

The man looked puzzled. "What strange tongue do you people speak?"

"Modern English," said Sarah. "Tell me, what is the name of the king?"

" 'Tis a stupid thing to ask," said the man. "All people know the name of the king."

"But we don't," said the Doctor. "At least, not your king. Think of us as strangers in your land. Who is your king?"

"Richard, but he's in the Holy Land, fighting the Infidel. John rules now."

31

"Good gracious," cried the Doctor. "We're not only dealing with reptiles that died out millions of years ago. This man has just stepped right out of the Middle Ages!"

3

The Time Eddy

At UNIT's temporary Headquarters in the classroom, the Brigadier and Sergeant Benton stood watching the radio operator as another report came in about the sighting of a monster.

"The signal's very faint, sir." The radio operator turned up the volume control on his console to "full." "It's no good, sir. They've faded out altogether."

The Brigadier had noticed that this always happened. There must be some connection between the appearance of the monsters and his radio operator's inability to pick up signals from the military mobile patrols.

"Did you hear anything?" he asked.

The radio operator turned to the Brigadier. "Only that one of the big flesh-eaters had stopped a truck taking two prisoners to one of the detention centers, sir. I think they said the prisoners escaped."

"I can hardly blame them." The Brigadier turned away.

"But they are villains, sir," protested Sergeant Benton. "I mean to say, any civilian in the Central Zone must be there for the pickings. We have to stop the looting."

"So I keep being told," snapped the Brigadier, returning to his desk, "by General Finch, and now by special dispatches from the Government. What they all forget is the main problem. We seem to be far more

33

interested in capturing petty crooks than slaughtering monsters." He glanced across at Benton's desk where the "in" tray was piled high with dispatches recently received. "You'd better get on with your filing, Sergeant."

"Yes, sir." Benton said and obediently returned to his desk.

The Brigadier sat down at his own desk. As an officer he was supposed to set a good example of leadership and hard work. At this moment in his career he had no idea where to lead anyone, and could think of no work that he could usefully do. It had been so much easier when he was fighting reptile men in the caves of Derbyshire, or even trying to exterminate giant maggots that came up from a disused mine in Wales. In both instances, the enemy was tangible and permanent. With these giant reptiles, he had no idea at all where they came from; even worse, he didn't know where they went. In every instance when his troops had pursued a monster it had gone behind buildings—and, by the time his troops turned the corner, the monster had vanished as though it never existed. He earnestly wished that the Doctor had not gone off on one of his jaunts into Time and Space.

"Sir!"

The excited voice of Sergeant Benton interrupted the Brigadier's thoughts. He looked up.

"What is it, Sergeant?"

"Look, sir." Benton was holding a photograph of the Doctor before the Brigadier's eyes.

"Very good, Benton. Pin it on the wall as a souvenir, and we can all wish he was here."

"But he is, sir," Benton persisted. "It's a mug shot from one of the Army posts. Listen to this." Benton read from an official paper. " ' Found accompanied by

34

a young woman in possession of stolen furs and a stolen van.' "

The Brigadier sprang to his feet. "The Doctor's been arrested as a looter?!"

"That's right, sir. And Sarah Jane Smith with him. They're being held, or *were* being held, at Number Five reception area."

The Brigadier hurried across the classroom to the radio operator. "Get Number Five reception area on the R/T."

The radio operator shook his head. "Can't do it, sir. The interference is too bad. Must be more monsters about, sir."

"All right, then," said the Brigadier. "I'll go myself. Sergeant Benton, I don't know what the Doctor thinks he's playing at, but he's going to have to answer to me!"

The Brigadier marched out of the classroom.

The Doctor smiled at the peasant from the Middle Ages. He was acutely aware of the man's fear—and the knife clutched in his hand.

"Tell me, old chap, can you remember what happened to you?"

" 'Tis a curse of the witches."

"Quite probably," replied the Doctor, wishing to sound agreeable. "But what were you doing when . . . when *it* happened?"

"I were doing no harm to God nor Man," said the peasant. "I were about to slaughter a pig with this knife."

Sarah recoiled. "Perhaps this is a vengeance on you for killing a poor defenseless animal."

The peasant glared at her. " 'Tis no crime to slaughter swine," he roared. "I have always been a good man, paying the tithes, tilling my master's land three days of

35

the week, and my own for three days. I go to church on Sundays and have my children christened."

"But you also believe in witches," said the Doctor.

"They cast spells against good Christian folk," said the peasant. "Be a friend, wizard, and take the curse off me."

"Unfortunately I can't," confessed the Doctor. "You see, I'm not a wizard—"

The man, without listening to the rest of the Doctor's sentence, raised his knife high above his head. "Then I'll slaughter you as I would that pig!"

As the peasant lunged forward with the rusted knife, the Doctor jumped back, tripping and falling. Sarah flung herself at the peasant, trying to grapple with him. All at once, as the knife was poised to slice into the Doctor's throat, Sarah felt a strange force pulling her back to where she had been standing. At the same time, the peasant went backward until he also was exactly where he had been standing. Then, as Sarah watched, the peasant became transparent—and disappeared.

The Doctor staggered to his feet. "Are you all right?"

"Are *you* all right?" she asked in return.

The Doctor felt his throat, and grinned. "He never touched me."

"I can't understand what happened," she said, "I went backward—and so did he. *Everything* seemed to go backward."

"Fascinating," commented the Doctor, brushing down his frock coat. "A Time eddy. Just for a moment, Time went into reverse."

"That's impossible, Time can only go forward."

"Are you sure of that?" queried the Doctor.

"It's the only way I can think," she said, lamely.

"Then let me stretch your thinking a little," said the Doctor. "Light travels at about 186,000 miles per second. Right?"

36

"Everyone knows that."

"I imagine our friend from the Middle Ages didn't know that," continued the Doctor with a smile, "but let that pass. If you are looking at a distant star, you may be looking at it as it *was* at the time of the birth of Jesus. If that star, or sun, has a planet and there are people living on it with a telescope strong enough to observe events on Earth, what would they see?"

Sarah got the point. "The Romans invading Britain. But that doesn't explain people and animals appearing from the past."

"No," said the Doctor, "but it puts to question the idea that Time is inflexible. On your planet, it was that chap Einstein who began to realize what was happening. Time, you see, moves at different speeds in different parts of the Universe. If I can find something to write on, let me show you some equations . . ."

The Doctor looked about for something to write with. But Sarah's attention was focused on sounds coming from the mews outside.

"I think you'll have to continue the lecture tomorrow," she whispered. "I'm sure that's soldiers outside—probably looking for us."

The Doctor listened. Nailed boots were clattering on the cobblestones beyond the big double doors. "I think you're right," he said. "I'll try to bolt the door."

He hurried over to the big double doors and looked desperately for some means to hold them fast. The approaching footsteps had now reached immediately outside, and someone was trying the handle of the door through which the Doctor and Sarah had entered.

"Hide!" The Doctor called across the garage to Sarah in an urgent whisper. She quickly hid behind some of the machinery.

The Doctor poised himself by the door to attack whoever might enter. Suddenly the door flung open and

37

a khaki-clad figure stepped into the garage. The Doctor moved forward to apply Venusian karate to the intruder's neck.

The Brigadier, aware someone was approaching him from behind, turned to face the Doctor, whose hands were poised ready for his neck.

"Good grief, Doctor," he said calmly, "whatever do you think you're playing at?"

"I was just about to render you unconscious," grinned the Doctor.

"So I gathered. If you can resist the temptation, perhaps you'd be good enough to accompany me back to our temporary Headquarters. We're having a bit of bother with prehistoric monsters popping up. You should be just the person we need to help sort out the mess."

The Doctor regarded the classroom which had been taken over by UNIT. "Is this the best you could do, Brigadier?"

"We have everything we need. A school provides plenty of rooms, toilet facilities, and a big kitchen. And with all London's children gone, no one was using it. Would you care to take a seat?"

But the Doctor had become too interested in the map of London that covered the blackboard. "What do all the flags mean?"

Sergeant Benton stepped forward to explain. "It's a color code, Doctor. Red flags for the sightings of a tyrannosaurus, blue for a triceratops, green for your stegosaurus, and pink for the pterodactyls."

"You've had all those different types of monsters?" Sarah asked.

"Those are the ones we know about," replied the Brigadier. He turned to the Doctor. "We soon realized that these giant reptiles only appeared in Central London. The Government therefore ordered the evacuation of the entire area."

"Apart from evacuating millions of people," said the Doctor, "and chasing after looters—"

"And arresting innocent people," Sarah cut in.

"—what," continued the Doctor, "have you actually *done*?"

"When these creatures appear," replied the Brigadier, "we try to make sure that they keep within the evacuated area and do not wander off into populated areas beyond the boundary of this line." He pointed to a heavy red line on the map that ringed Central London.

"But having contained them in this way," continued the Doctor, "what do you *do*?"

The Brigadier smiled. "That's where you come in, Doctor. We've no idea where they come from, or where they vanish to. In fact that really puzzles me—the way they just seem to disappear."

"I should think the explanation is pretty simple," said the Doctor. "They return to where they came from. The past."

General Finch marched into the classroom, followed by Captain Yates. Sarah took an instant dislike to the General, but warmed when she saw young Captain Yates of UNIT. Sergeant Benton leapt to attention. The Brigadier straightened his shoulders and turned to greet his superior officer.

"All right, Brigadier," the General's voice boomed, "I've arranged for the extra patrols you want. But I warn you, I shall expect results."

Ignoring the General, the Doctor went forward to shake Captain Yates's hand. "My dear Yates," he grinned, "how nice to see you again. How are you?" Only recently, when UNIT and the Doctor had been battling against an artificially created outbreak of giant maggots in Wales, Captain Yates had been captured by

39

a group of villains and mentally "readjusted" so that he would do their bidding. At their orders he had almost murdered his good friend the Doctor, but his own conscience had prevented him from carrying out the order at the last moment. Although the Doctor had eventually helped Yates recover control of his own mind, it was generally believed that the young Captain had undergone terrific mental strain. He was given a very long leave in which to get better.

"I'm fine now," said Captain Yates, "thanks to you."

General Finch, who did not like being ignored at any time, turned and stared at the Doctor. "Who is this man?"

"This is the Doctor, sir," said the Brigadier, "our scientific adviser."

"We've all been waiting for you to show up. May I ask where you've been?" said the General.

"Certainly," replied the Doctor.

There was an awkward silence. The General realized the Doctor was making a fool of him.

"Well?" he rapped.

"You may ask," replied the Doctor, "but I don't intend to give an answer, not if you speak to me in that tone of voice."

The Brigadier stepped in quickly. "Doctor, this is General Finch. He has overall charge of this entire operation."

"Really?" said the Doctor. He smiled disarmingly and extended his hand to the now red-faced General. "How do you do? I'm terribly pleased to meet you."

Before the General could utter a word, the Brigadier spoke rapidly. "The Doctor's already come up with a most interesting theory, sir. He believes that these creatures are coming to us from the past."

The General touched his closely cropped moustache. "Very interesting. How?"

The Brigadier turned back to the Doctor. "That's a good point, Doctor. How do they do it?"

"Somebody or something," said the Doctor airily, "is causing temporal displacement on a massive scale."

"Temporal displacement?" queried the Brigadier, not understanding the terminology.

"Putting it another way," continued the Doctor, "someone is mucking about with Time."

"Rubbish," said the General. "Absolute nonsense!"

"I take it you have a better theory, General?"

The General cleared his throat noisily. "Some mad scientist fellow has been secretly breeding these things. Now they've escaped."

Sarah piped up, "That wouldn't account for the man from the Middle Ages we met in the garage!"

General Finch turned and stared at Sarah, as though he hadn't noticed her before. "Who is this person?"

"Sarah Jane Smith. I'm a journalist."

The General swung back to face the Brigadier. "No journalists are allowed in this zone. Have her evacuated immediately."

"Miss Smith is acting as my assistant, General," the Doctor turned to her. "You were saying, my dear?"

Sarah quickly told of their encounter with the peasant from the time of King John. "Don't you see, General," she concluded, "it's not only reptiles, it's people. Maybe *anything* will pop up from the past now."

The General rocked on his heels, his favorite stance. He tapped his leg with his swagger cane. "Have you never heard of mentally deranged people believing they were Napoleon? I suggest your so-called peasant was mad."

"He vanished before Miss Smith's very eyes," said the Doctor. "Madmen can't do that."

From his radio console, the operator turned excitedly

41

to Sergeant Benton. "Another sighting, Sarge. Just come through."

In a flash Benton went to take the note the radio operator had scribbled down while listening to reports of the new sighting.

"Where is it?" asked the Brigadier.

Benton helped himself to a green flag from a little cardboard box on the desk top, and stuck it carefully on the map. "There, sir," he said. "It's a stegosaurus this time."

"Get on to the artillery right away," the General ordered the Brigadier. "We need field guns to blast it into eternity."

The Doctor stepped forward. He was a good six inches taller than the General. "You'll do no such thing! We must study that creature, not shoot at it. How much do you think we'll learn from a dead dinosaur?" He took the Brigadier's arm. "Come on, Brigadier, I want you to get me there as quickly as possible."

The Brigadier looked startled. "What do you intend to do? Make friends with it?"

"Possibly," said the Doctor. "But first we've got to catch it."

The stegosaurus, thirty feet long and weighing two tons, stood bewildered in a narrow Hampstead side street. In the distance it could see the green of Hampstead Heath, and the prospect of so much lush foliage made its salivic juices run. But immediately ahead was a little group of mammalian midgets colored brown, and they were frightening because they carried sticks that made big bangs. Each time one of the sticks banged, the stegosaurus's nerve center set in its hip reacted to pin pricks of pain. No doubt a tyrannosaurus or a pterodactyl would have enjoyed the little mammals, as a between-meals snack, but the stegosaurus longed only to munch peacefully on big green leaves. It wished the little mammals would all go away. In anguish at being trapped in this uninviting valley, it swished its tail. The fronts of three houses shattered and crumbled with a roar of falling bricks and masonry. As the dust cleared, the three houses looked like dolls' houses with the front taken away—each floor left intact with the furniture now exposed to view.

The jeep which was carrying the Doctor and the Brigadier screeched to a halt. A UNIT corporal ran forward and saluted.

"Corporal Norton, sir!"

The Brigadier jumped down from the jeep. "What's the situation, Corporal?"

"As you can see, sir, we're containing the steggi in this street."

The Doctor raised his eyebrows. "The *steggi*?"

"We had to shorten their names," explained the Brigadier. "This Latin scientific stuff got a bit beyond some of my men."

"Whatever you call it," said the Doctor, "it's a remarkable specimen. I must get a better look." He strode toward the great mound of armor-plated flesh that blocked the little street.

"Do be careful!" called the Brigadier.

"It's all right. These things were vegetarians."

The stegosaurus was backing further and further into the street. It swished its tail in fear, totally destroying two more houses.

"It's causing terrible damage to private property," the Brigadier shouted. "We'll have to lay charges under it and try to kill it."

"Don't be so bloodthirsty. What we need are ropes and a strong net." The Doctor returned to the jeep.

43

"If you insist," said the Brigadier reluctantly. "Corporal, what ropes have we got?"

"There are towing ropes in all the vehicles, sir," replied the incredulous corporal. "If we catch it, how are we going to move it, sir?"

"Good point!" The Brigadier turned to the Doctor. "How indeed, eh?"

"One thing at a time," said the Doctor. "If we can rope its legs together, that will stop it moving. Then we could get one of those giant trucks they use for transporting heavy equipment. I want to get it somewhere quiet so that I can observe it under laboratory conditions."

"And what if it struggles?"

"That's one of the many risks we shall have to take. But it may be quite docile. Its brain is only the size of a walnut."

"We'll give it a try then," said the Brigadier. "Corporal, get all the towing ropes we have to hand—and tell your men to be careful. One swish of that tail and they'll be squashed like jelly."

"Sir!" said the corporal, saluting smartly. He hurried away to the Army vehicles standing close by.

"I don't mind telling you," said the Brigadier, "that in my opinion this is a lunatic scheme . . ."

The Brigadier suddenly froze, as though Time was standing still. The Doctor turned quickly to look at the stegosaurus. The huge reptile was already transparent, and in a moment had vanished. From the corner of his eye, the Doctor saw the corporal *running backward* toward them. He looked now at the Brigadier. The Brigadier blinked, and cleared his throat as the corporal returned to stand in front of him.

"Tell your men to be careful," said the Brigadier. "One swish of that tail and they'll be squashed like jelly—" The Brigadier stopped mid-sentence. "It's gone! It's disappeared!"

The corporal turned to look. "Blimey, sir. How did that happen?"

Sergeant Benton placed two mugs of tea on a desk top next to Captain Yates and Sarah. "Thought I'd brew tea, sir, while the others are chasing after that steggi."

"Very kind of you," said Yates.

Benton smiled and left discreetly.

"You were telling me about Wales," Sarah said.

"After all that business with the giant maggots, I had to have a spot of leave."

"*Had* to?"

"The people who created the maggots put me under some hypnotic spell." He smiled, very charmingly Sarah thought. "Lot of nonsense, really. Anyway, I'm all right now."

"I hope so." Sarah took her steaming mug of tea over to one of the classroom windows and looked out. "It's weird seeing London like this—all these deserted streets."

"I rather like it," he said. "Have you noticed how clean the air's become? No cars, no people. Only yesterday I saw a fox in Piccadilly."

She turned and laughed. "And nightingales singing in Berkeley Square?" She was referring to an old and very sentimental song from the years of the Second World War.

Captain Yates did not laugh in return. He spoke quite seriously. "It's not impossible. Nature is always ready and waiting to take back the places that humans have despoiled."

"I like London the way it was," said Sarah. "Traffic jams, pollution and all."

45

"I suppose you do." Yates picked up his own mug of tea and stared into its steamy surface. "Perhaps I'm a bit old-fashioned."

Sarah looked hard at him. What could be going on in his mind?

General Finch, red-faced and angry, was facing the Doctor across the classroom.

"Disappeared?" scoffed the General. "You must mean *you* disappeared when it got too close!"

"What reason had I to be frightened? It was a herbivore."

"A *what*?"

"A vegetarian, sir," explained the Brigadier. Sarah, Captain Yates and Sergeant Benton were watching the clash between the General and the Doctor with mounting interest.

The General swung round to face the Brigadier. "I should like to know what role you played in this fiasco. How did you lose it?"

"I've no idea, sir. One moment we were getting towing ropes to capture it, and the next it was gone. Vanished into thin air."

The General's eyes narrowed. "You *saw* it vanish?"

The Brigadier, who couldn't remember exactly what he had seen, hesitated. The Doctor stepped forward. "The Brigadier and his men didn't *see* what happened. They were temporarily affected by a Time eddy. You see, General, these creatures are being moved back and forth through Time."

The General's face grew redder. "Ridiculous!"

The Doctor continued calmly. "Whenever a creature appears or disappears, the temporal displacement produces a localized distortion in Time. As far as people immediately in the areas are concerned, Time literally flows backward. In fact, one of the UNIT corporals

46

started to run backward. Naturally, they have no memory of what has occurred."

The Brigadier smiled and tried to soothe the bad-tempered General. "Suppose, sir, that we accept the Doctor's theory for the sake of discussion." He turned to the Doctor. "What's the next step?"

"We must capture one of these creatures."

"What good will that do?" asked the General.

"I shall explain." The Doctor crossed to the map of London on the blackboard. "Someone must be causing these apparitions, General. I intend to track them down." He pointed to the map. "Why are reptiles only appearing in this one small area?"

"I would hardly call the whole of Central London a small area!" retorted the General.

"But the giant reptiles flourished everywhere on this planet. So why aren't they popping up everywhere?"

"I say," said the Brigadier, "that's a jolly good point!"

"Could I ask something, Doctor?" chipped in Sarah.

"Yes, my dear. What is it?"

"What about the man we saw in the garage?"

"I think he was an accident—or an early experiment." The Doctor pointed to the ringed area on the map. He spoke with mounting conviction. "Somebody is deliberately causing these phenomena—and they're operating from the middle of London!"

For a moment no one spoke. Captain Yates broke the silence. "You're overlooking one important point, Doctor. The whole of Central London has been evacuated. The military, and a few stray looters, are the only people living in the entire area."

"The only ones we know about," replied the Doctor. "I can assure you that somebody is causing this to happen, and if my theories are correct, they must be using massive amounts of electricity."

47

The General smirked. "By that idiotic remark alone, you defeat your own argument. All electricity supplies have been cut off in Central London."

"Thank you, General. In that case, they must be making their own!"

4

The Timescoop

Professor Whitaker peered at the massive control console of the Timescoop, and smiled inwardly at his achievement.

In the entire history of Humankind, he was the only person ever to have changed Time. Others had climbed Everest and launched people into Space—but only Professor Whitaker had moved things, people, and prehistoric monsters through Time!

Many problems, however, remained to be solved. The Timescoop had twice gone out of control—once removing a startled Roman soldier from the midst of a battle into Trafalgar Square, and once scooping up a medieval peasant. . . . But these were small errors compared with the technological magnificence of being able to focus the "scoop" onto a particular dinosaur at a precise moment in pre-history and to bring it safely into the present.

It crossed his mind that if he had the Time (he smiled at his own pun) he could hobnob with any number of famous people from the past. He could, if he wished, summon up Henry VIII, although the King's Old English would be difficult to understand. Perhaps Oscar Wilde would be more fun to meet, or perhaps the late Noël Coward. Some of the great mysteries of the past, such as the disappearance of the two princes in the Tower, could be solved by the Timescoop.

Yet although he could manipulate Time, it was the one thing he was short of. The people he worked with were always pressing him to complete the Timescoop. If only they weren't in such a hurry.

A technician called across the control room. "Power output holding steady at one million volts, Professor."

"Thank you," he called back.

Butler, a man he disliked, came over to him. "The next Time-transference is due in one hour, Professor."

Whitaker turned away and busied himself adjusting some controls. He'd never liked the look of the jagged scar that ran down Butler's left cheek. "It may have to wait."

"We must maintain the Time-transference schedule," said Butler. "The sequence has been carefully calculated."

Whitaker swung round. "How can I work on the main project when I have these constant distractions?"

Butler put on his awful smile. "These distractions, Professor, have emptied London for us. We must keep the authorities off balance."

Whitaker tried to avoid looking at the jagged scar. "What's the weather like up above?"

Butler was surprised by the question. "Does it affect the program in any way?"

"You know very well it doesn't. I just wondered if it was raining. I haven't seen daylight for a month."

"If it really interests you, Professor, I shall try to find out. But may I first ask if we shall have the next transference on time?"

Whitaker turned back to his console. "I suppose so. But don't blame me if the final countdown is delayed." He began making rapid calculations on a miniaturized computer, and paused when he realized that Butler was still standing behind him. Without turning, he said, "Well, what is it now?"

"The final countdown mustn't be delayed, Professor," said Butler's voice. "You are aware of that. Everything depends on you."

At last Butler was showing some sense. Of course everything depended on the brilliance and genius of Professor Whitaker. He liked it when other people acknowledged this fact.

"I shall do my best," he said. "Now will you please stop standing behind me? It puts me off."

"Certainly," said Butler.

Whitaker's well-manicured finger jabbed two more digits on the miniaturized computer, then he stole a glance over his shoulder. Butler had moved away and was reading power input dials. Whitaker thought it was such a pity about that awful scar.

At UNIT's temporary Headquarters the Doctor had rigged up the headmaster's office as a private workshop. Captain Yates watched as the Doctor wired the main circuit of the stun-gun he'd just completed—a long-barreled weapon with shoulder pad, sights and a trigger.

"You really think you can knock out a dinosaur with that thing?" asked Yates.

"Naturally," said the Doctor, continuing with his work, and wishing Yates would go away.

"How?"

"Relative velocity of molecular reaction," replied the Doctor, knowing that Captain Yates would not understand a word.

"I see."

"No you don't." The Doctor paused, looked up, and grinned. "The principle hasn't been developed on Earth yet."

Captain Yates examined the weapon closely. "What exactly will it *do*?"

"It'll temporarily neutralize the creature's brain cells," answered the Doctor patiently.

Yates frowned. "I thought these creatures hadn't any brains."

"All animals have a brain of some sort. Dinosaurs' brains are particularly small compared with their over-all size. In fact, the modern kitten has more brains than the largest dinosaurs ever had."

"So what'll happen to the dinosaur when you switch that thing on?"

"Its brain will be affected by a directional beam carrying a small power charge."

"Then what?"

"It'll faint."

"What will you do with your monster once it's fainted?"

The Doctor put down the gun. He realized he wouldn't be able to get on with any more work while Captain Yates was there. "I'll surround it with an electrical field, and wait for it to disappear into the past."

"Is that going to tell us anything?"

"With any luck I shall discover the source of the power which is moving these creatures through Time."

"Will it be accurate enough?"

"I hope so. It'll be like the way in which triangulation's used to detect radio transmitters. I think it'll be accurate enough for the Brigadier to send a squad of men to round up the guilty parties."

"Jolly good," said Captain Yates, putting on his cap. "Well, if you can spare me, I'll let you get on with it, Doctor."

"That would be most helpful," said the Doctor, eager to continue his work.

Yates opened the door to leave and Sarah rushed through it.

"Doctor," she gasped, "that General Finch is being impossible—" She stopped mid-sentence when she saw the Doctor's weapon. "What are you making?"

The Doctor again tried to get on with his work. "Ask Captain Yates, my dear. Now will you please leave me in peace!"

Feeling rejected, Sarah turned to the handsome young Captain. "That wretched General of yours is trying to have me evacuated out of London."

"You're a civilian, Sarah. You have no official status."

"That's stupid," she replied in annoyance. "Doctor, I'm your assistant, aren't I?"

The Doctor was attaching the terminals of the main electrical circuit of the stun-gun, a delicate operation. "Yes, yes, my dear," he called, without looking Sarah's way. "Anything you like."

"There you are," Sarah said to Captain Yates. "So I have a right to be here."

Yates gave her a quizzical look. "Tell you what, I'll fix you up with a temporary pass. Just stay out of sight of General Finch." He smiled, and hurried away.

Sarah came forward to take a closer look at the Doctor's work. "What did you say that thing is, Doctor?"

"I didn't."

"Can I help at all?"

"No."

"If I'm supposed to be your assistant, there must be something I can do."

"There is," said the Doctor. "Go away."

"You'd really sooner be left alone, wouldn't you?"

"How ever did you guess, my dear?"

Sarah said, "I can take a hint." She tiptoed out of the temporary workshop.

The Doctor sighed with relief, bolted the door, and

53

tried to get on with his work. As he returned to his work bench there was a tap on the door.

"Go away," he called. "There's no one in here."

The Brigadier spoke through the bolted door. "May I see you, please? We have a very important visitor."

"*I* am a very important visitor," the Doctor called back through the door.

"Very funny," said the Brigadier. "But standing outside here with me is a member of the Government."

Reluctantly the Doctor put down the stun-gun and unbolted the door. Standing outside with the Brigadier was a short intelligent-looking man in his fifties wearing an expensively cut lounge suit. His politician's smile turned on the Doctor.

"This is the Doctor, sir," the Brigadier told the visitor. "Doctor, let me introduce Sir Charles Grover, Minister with Special Powers."

Grover's smile, seen frequently on millions of television sets, continued. "I do apologize for the interruption, Doctor. I realize how busy you are."

"I'm glad somebody does," replied the Doctor without trying to conceal the grumpiness in his voice. "Anyway, come in."

Grover stepped into the headmaster's office. "The Brigadier tells me that you may find the solution to this appalling crisis."

"I hope so." The Doctor took a closer look at Grover. "Aren't you the chap who started the Save Planet Earth Society?"

"I had a little to do with its founding," said Grover, modestly.

The Doctor continued, "And you wrote that book, *Last Chance for Man,* didn't you?"

"That's right, ably assisted by my colleagues, of course, who did so much of the research."

The Doctor extended his hand. "My dear chap, I'm

very pleased to meet you. This planet needs people like you."

To the Brigadier's relief, the Doctor and the Cabinet Minister shook hands warmly. He recalled that the Save Planet Earth Society, which sought to predict what life on Earth would be like in the future, had once been regarded as a bunch of cranks; they were now taken very seriously indeed.

"You two have a great deal in common, if I may say so. The Doctor's very keen on this anti-pollution business," said the Brigadier.

"And so should you be, Brigadier," replied Grover. "It affects all our lives." He turned back to the Doctor. "Tell me, Doctor, do you have any theories on why all this is happening?"

"I believe the dinosaurs are being used purely as a weapon of terror, to clear Central London."

Grover looked astounded. "You mean people are *doing* this?"

"Although the speed of Time may vary in different parts of the Universe as a whole," continued the Doctor, "the chances of a localized Time-slip occurring as a result through natural causes are extremely rare. Yes, Sir Charles, people are doing it."

"But why?"

The Doctor paused. "I take it that everything I say to you is in strict confidence?"

The Brigadier spoke up. "Doctor, Sir Charles represents the Government. We have no secrets from our superiors." It was a gentle reminder to the Doctor that he nowadays worked for UNIT.

"Of course not," said the Doctor blandly. "My belief is that the people responsible for bringing these creatures into the present want to clear London of its population. They have some vast project that can only be carried out in a deserted London."

Charles Grover looked puzzled. "But why London? If they wanted wide-open depopulated areas, why not choose the Yorkshire Moors or the Highlands of Scotland?"

"Why indeed?" said the Doctor. "Obviously there must be some overriding reason, something they need that is only available to them here."

Sergeant Benton rushed into the office. He ignored Sir Charles Grover, briefly acknowledged the Brigadier, and went straight up to the Doctor. "They've just spotted one, Doctor. Section Twelve."

"Do you know what kind it is?"

Benton looked at a chit of paper in his hand. "Apato something."

"Apatosaurus," said the Doctor, "more commonly known as the brontosaurus. Large, placid, and stupid. Exactly what we need."

"May I ask what's going on?" asked Sir Charles.

"This is a stun-gun." The Doctor indicated the weapon on the makeshift work bench. "It is imperative that we catch one of these creatures, and I may be able to do it with this." He swung round to the Brigadier. "Can I have transport laid on straight away?"

"Of course," replied the Brigadier. "Benton, see to it."

"Already done, sir."

"Then let's go," said the Doctor. "There's no time to lose." He paused at the door. "Excuse our sudden departure, Sir Charles, we'll keep you informed."

The Doctor, the Brigadier and Sergeant Benton hurried out, leaving Sir Charles Grover on his own. He looked around the headmaster's office. He remembered when he was master in a grammar school, long before he went into politics. They were happy days when the future seemed full of hope. He wished he could have that Time over again.

In the control center, deep below London, Butler saw a light flashing. It meant someone was using the elevator. He found this curious since they did not expect visitors at this time. He hurried out of the control room, down the corridor to the elevators. The indicator confirmed that someone was descending. He waited for the doors to open. It was young Captain Yates.

Butler said, "You're never supposed to come here."

"It's urgent," said Yates. "Where's Professor Whitaker?"

"Playing with his Timescoop," said Butler. "This way."

Butler led the young captain along the corridor to the control room. On entering, Yates looked about himself, very impressed by all the gleaming scientific equipment.

"Over here," Butler called.

Yates crossed to where Professor Whitaker was adjusting countrols on the Timescoop. The Professor looked up. His sickly smile always turned Yates's stomach.

"Dear boy," said Whitaker, "how lovely to see you—"

"The Doctor's back," Yates blurted out, interrupting him.

"Really? And who, may I ask, is the Doctor?"

"UNIT's scientific adviser," replied Yates, his face grim. "The one person who could catch us."

"I wish you wouldn't use words like that. You make us sound like common criminals."

Butler cut in. "I think you should listen to Captain Yates, Professor. This may be important."

The Professor turned on his swivel chair to face Yates. "Do carry on, Captain."

"The Doctor is making a stun-gun to catch one of the monsters," Yates continued. "Once he's got one he intends to surround it with an electrical field and then wait for it to disappear. In some way, I don't understand how, that will give away the location of the Timescoop."

Whitaker laced his fingers and looked down at the well-polished nails. "Most ingenious. And most improbable."

"If the Doctor says he can do it," said Yates, "I believe him. He's probably the most brilliant scientist on this planet."

"That," said Whitaker, looking up sharply, "is a matter of opinion."

"But don't you realize what will happen if he's right? It'll be the end of Operation Golden Age. Everything we've planned will be ruined."

"Well," said Whitaker after a few moments' thought, "you're the soldier. You'd better do something about this Doctor of yours."

"I'll do nothing to harm him, nor will I allow him to be harmed by anyone else. If we descend to that sort of thing we're no better than the society we're trying to get away from."

"How very touching," said the Professor. "Then what do you propose we do,"

Yates hesitated. "I'm afraid I have no idea."

"Naturally," scoffed Professor Whitaker. "I'm the one who has to come up with all the ideas. So now I shall contribute yet another brilliant inspiration—for the good of the cause. We must sabotage this so-called stun-gun."

"How?"

"It won't be difficult." The Professor rose from his swivel chair. "Give me a few minutes at the work bench and I shall produce the very thing for you."

"For me?" queried Yates.

"Of course, dear boy. You'll have to deliver the goods. But don't worry, it'll only affect the stun-gun. I

58

shall see that not a hair of your precious Doctor's head is harmed."

The Brigadier's jeep screamed to a stop. He gazed in awe at the monster which the soldiers were holding at bay. Long as a railway coach and thirty tons in bulk, the giant, fully grown brontosaurus filled the little street next to a factory.

"What a remarkable specimen," said the Doctor as he climbed out of the jeep. He carefully laid the cumbersome stun-gun on the back seat. "Let's take a closer look."

Cautiously, the Brigadier and the Doctor walked toward the towering monster. Its head, high as a three-story house, swung to and fro on the end of its long neck: it was trying to get the humans into focus.

"How convenient," remarked the Doctor, "to have it turn up in a cul-de-sac. It can't escape."

"Is this the kind you wanted, Doctor?" the Brigadier asked with a shiver.

"The bigger the better," replied the Doctor, rubbing his hands together. "The larger the mass, the greater the temporal displacement."

"What's the firing range of that stun-gun of yours?" asked the Brigadier.

"I shall have to get up quite close," said the Doctor. "But not to worry. These fellows aren't partial to flesh." He gazed at the monster's head towering above him. "He got that big by munching soft plants."

Another jeep screeched to a halt. Captain Yates stepped out. "Anything I can do, Doctor?"

"You could get my stun-gun," the Doctor called back.

The captain ran to the Brigadier's parked jeep. As he picked up the weapon, he took a small metallic disc from the palm of his hand and pushed it into position under the barrel. It would, Professor Whitaker had assured him, neutralize the stun-gun without endangering the Doctor.

"You carry the gun," Yates told a soldier. "I'll take the power pack." Yates picked up the rucksack which contained nothing more than high-voltage batteries attached to the stun-gun. Together they carried the apparatus to where the Doctor was standing.

"Thank you," said the Doctor. "Now, someone help me on with the power pack."

With Captain Yates's help the Doctor struggled into the rucksack, and then took the gun from the soldier.

The Brigadier called to his soldiers, "Stand by with covering fire if necessary!"

"It won't be necessary," smiled the Doctor. "These things don't bite. Five minutes from now we shall have a very unconscious brontosaurus on our hands."

The Doctor walked forward into the cul-de-sac. The reptile turned its head again, focusing on the midget now approaching. It backed away, its vast whiplash tail pushing down a high brick wall at the end of the street. The Doctor stopped when he was directly under the monster's head. Satisfying himself that the stun-gun had been correctly adjusted, he took careful aim and pulled the trigger. Nothing happened. The Doctor examined the controls, made a finer adjustment, took aim, and fired again. Still no response from the stun-gun. Suddenly, the Doctor heard a great roar of anger from behind him. He spun round. Blocking the exit from the street towered a thirty-foot-high tyrannosaurus rex, its savage jaws dripping with the blood of some prey it had just killed, before being hurtled through a hundred and fifty million years of Time.

The Brigadier blinked. "What happened?" For a fraction of a second, Time had stood still for him.

"That monster," shouted Captain Yates, "it must

have suddenly appeared. I must save the Doctor. It's a killer!"

Yates drew his service revolver and ran toward the tyrannosaurus rex.

"Yates," called the Brigadier, "come back. We can't fire on it with you there!"

But Captain Yates ignored the Brigadier. He worked his way round the giant's foot, hoping to get a shot at its head. Rounding the base of the monster, he saw that the brontosaurus had vanished. The Doctor had tripped, and lay stunned on the ground. The tyrannosaurus rex was lowering its blooded jaws to eat the Doctor. Captain Yates fired twice at the monster's head, hitting the huge jaw with the second bullet. The reptile raised its head, as though angered by the bite of a fly. In that moment Captain Yates threw himself across the narrow street, landing beside the discarded stun-gun. He ripped off the concealed metallic disc, grabbed the stun-gun, and rolled over on to his back. Aiming the sights at the monster's towering head, he pulled the trigger. The stun-gun sizzled with the power flowing through it. Instantly the monster staggered. Yates blasted it again. The tyrannosaurus rex, the most feared animal which had ever lived, leaned drunkenly against the wall of the factory, its little two-fingered hands flaying the air hopelessly. Captain Yates scrambled to his feet, grabbed the Doctor under his arms and pulled him to safety, just as the reptile crumpled forward in a dead faint.

5

Monster in Chains

"You tried to murder the Doctor!"

Captain Yates was standing over Professor Whitaker, shaking with anger. "You deliberately materialized a savage monster knowing full well it would attack the Doctor!"

Butler, his scar more livid than usual, spoke up. "An unavoidable mistake, Captain Yates."

"It was deliberate," Yates stormed. "And you know it!"

"If I may be allowed to speak," said Professor Whitaker, "it was you, Captain Yates, who sabotaged the stun-gun."

"Only to stop the Doctor catching a monster, and certainly not so that you could turn a flesh-eater onto him!" He tried to speak more calmly. "Look, let me tell the Doctor what we're doing. I'm sure he'd be sympathetic. He might even try to help us."

Professor Whitaker's face hardened. "That's quite out of the question. What if he didn't agree with our aims?"

"But I'm sure he would," Yates pleaded. "Everything we are doing is for the good of Mankind." He paused. "It is, isn't it?"

Butler smiled. "Captain Yates, would *you* be involved if it were not? In the end we shall be judged the saviors of the human race. One cannot have ideals higher than that."

Yates felt reassured. "That's true," he said. "But there's no need to harm the Doctor."

Professor Whitaker smiled. "It's nice to see you care. I wouldn't mind meeting this Doctor myself sometime." Then he added quickly, "But not just now. Tell me, what stage has he reached?"

"They've taken the creature to an aircraft hangar on the fringe of the evacuated area. The Doctor's surrounding it with an electrical field. As I told you before, he intends to record when the monster vanishes in order to track down the location of this control center."

"Then more sabotage will be necessary," said Butler. "More work for you, Captain Yates."

"Sorry. Count me out."

Butler and Whitaker exchanged a quick glance. Butler continued, "We can't count you out, Captain Yates. Who else can do the sabotage except you?"

Yates thought about that. "All right. What do you want me to do?"

"Ensure that the Doctor's instruments don't work," said the Professor. "In due course, the creature will return to its own time. When that happens, the Doctor must *not* be able to locate the source of its temporal displacement."

"I'll do what I can," promised Yates, preparing to leave.

"Don't forget," added Butler, "that if the Doctor finds this place, it will mean the end of Operation Golden Age. The entire future of Man depends on you, Captain Yates."

Yates nodded, and hurried out.

Whitaker turned to Butler. "You forgot to mention the past of Man."

Butler, his back to the Professor, was studying a set

63

of instruments. "There are some things it's better for Captain Yates not to know."

The Brigadier and Sarah were standing in the hangar office gazing through an internal window at the Doctor as he walked the length of the tyrannosaurus. The giant reptile, still unconscious, and lying on its side, filled the aircraft hangar. Thick chains, attached to heavy spikes driven into the concrete floor, were padlocked round the creature's hind legs, tail and neck. A series of electrical antennae, rather like indoor television aerials, surrounded the monster. These antennae were linked by cables to an apparatus that the Doctor had hastily rigged up in the office.

"I hope it doesn't wake up," said Sarah.

"Don't worry," replied the Brigadier. "Those chains could hold a herd of wild elephants."

The Doctor, seeming satisfied with the arrangements in the hangar, returned to the office.

"Sleeping peacefully?" asked the Brigadier.

"Not exactly sleeping," said the Doctor, as he checked the dials and gauges of the directional detector, "but still in a faint. I wonder if those creatures ever dreamed?"

"What a curious fellow you are," laughed the Brigadier, "to think of something like that at a time like this."

"There's not much else to think about until the animal dematerializes." The Doctor adjusted some of the controls.

Sarah seized her opportunity. "Then perhaps I could tell you something, Doctor?"

"But of course," he murmured, his attention entirely focused on a small black knob that he kept twiddling. "I'm all ears."

Sarah glanced at the Brigadier. He shrugged and smiled an encouragement to her to continue.

"I've been investigating the whole question of Time travel," she said, hoping to gain his undivided attention.

"Have you?" He continued to turn the black knob to and fro. "You know, I think this could do with a spot of oil. You wouldn't have any handy, would you, Brigadier?"

"I don't usually carry it on me."

"Oh well, I suppose we can manage." The Doctor seemed to forget the troublesome black knob. He started tapping one of the dials to see if the finger inside would flicker. "You were talking about Time travel, Sarah."

"I thought you hadn't listened." Then she continued quickly: "One or two people have dabbled."

"Fascinating," said the Doctor. "The main difficulty is the Blinovitch Limitation Effect. Do you know about Blinovitch? A great bear of a man from Russia. At least he was until *he* dabbled. He put Time into reverse for himself. The last I heard of him he was reaching babyhood. Rather a waste, I think. He was a brilliant man— when he *was* a man."

Sarah persisted. "I think someone may have overcome that limitation."

The Doctor turned. "On this planet?"

"It's the only planet I've been able to check."

"Yes, of course. How foolish of me." The Doctor rubbed his nose thoughtfully. "I remember there was a Chinese scientist called Chun Sen . . . but he hasn't been born yet. And then there was a South American, but his name escapes me."

"There's a man called Whitaker," Sarah cut in. "He claimed to have developed a workable theory on Time travel."

The Brigadier snapped his fingers. "I remember! He applied for a big Government grant. It was refused."

"Why?" asked the Doctor. "Has the Government no interest in science?"

Sarah supplied the answer. "It was Whitaker himself who put them off. He was always quarreling with other scientists—so no one thought his theory would work."

"What a petty-minded lot!" exclaimed the Doctor.

"If I remember rightly," added the Brigadier, "the Government took advice on the theory. But all their scientific advisers said this fellow Whitaker was a crank."

"That is what people *always* say about anyone with a new idea," complained the Doctor.

"Quite so," agreed the Brigadier. He turned to Sarah. "Anyway, what about him?"

"He disappeared," she said flatly.

The Doctor now scratched his nose. This was becoming interesting. "Are you sure of that?"

"About six months ago. Professor Whitaker completely vanished. I've checked with everybody—the newspapers, the police, his friends. He hasn't been heard of for six whole months."

The Brigadier cleared his throat. "Not that I doubt a word for a minute, Miss Smith, but since all the newspapers, and the police and everyone else has fled London, how did you make your inquiries?"

She smiled disarmingly. "I spent rather a long time using the telephone in your office. STD is still working."

"Sarah, do you seriously think this man Whitaker could be behind it all?" The Doctor looked thoughtful.

"It's something I once read on how the police work," she explained. "If there's a murder or a robbery, they always look for any *odd* thing that happened at around that time. The man, for example, who always drives himself to work but on the day of the murder traveled by bus. Now here we've got someone playing around with Time, and six months ago the one man who claimed he could control Time vanished. And it's a fact that never before in his life did he go off without telling everyone of his whereabouts—you know, holidays, attending international conferences, and so on."

The Brigadier was clearly impressed. "This is a most extraordinary coincidence, don't you agree, Doctor?"

Before the Doctor could answer, Sarah concluded her argument. "You see, Doctor, he must have been bitterly disappointed when the Government refused to help him develop his theories. So what if he found other people who would put up the money and provide all the facilities he'd need?"

The Doctor was pensive for some moments. Then he began to speak rapidly. "I'd like to see this chap's working papers, Brigadier. Is that possible?"

"I suppose they must be somewhere, perhaps at his home, or filed by the Government when he made his application for help."

"Another thing," said the Doctor, "ask your UNIT chaps to transport the TARDIS to your temporary Headquarters. There are special instruments inside that I shall need."

"The order was given some hours ago. The TARDIS should be there by now."

"Good. Perhaps you could drive me over there."

"What about your little pet in the hangar?" asked Sarah.

The Doctor looked through the internal window at the enormous bulk of the green, leathery tyrannosaurus rex. "He'll be all right for a while." He turned to the Brigadier. "You'll post a guard?"

The Brigadier nodded. "General Finch has lent me a special squad."

"But what if it dematerializes while you're back at UNIT Headquarters?" Sarah asked.

"My instruments will still obtain the necessary readings. Are you going to come with us?"

"Yes," replied Sarah eagerly. "I must get my camera."

"Whatever for?" asked the Brigadier.

"I'm a journalist, remember. When all this is over, I want to write about it *and* have photographs to offer to newspapers. It'll be the scoop of a lifetime."

The Brigadier looked stern. "I'm sorry, Miss Smith, but this whole affair is under a strict security blackout. You can take your photographs once the crisis is over."

"But, Brigadier," she cried out, "when the crisis is over there won't be anything to photograph!"

"I'm sorry, Miss Smith," the Brigadier repeated firmly, "but those are my orders. Are you ready, Doctor?"

The Doctor and the Brigadier hurried out. Sarah, pouting a little, took one last look at the monster, then turned and followed.

Had Sarah remained behind one second more she might have seen the reptile's right eyelid blink. It was only a momentary flicker, as the reptile's minute brain was starting to regain consciousness. As often happens with humans when they recover from a faint, the tyrannosaurus rex had a very severe headache. It breathed deeply, then fell into a peaceful sleep.

Captain Yates quietly entered the office. For the past half hour he had been concealed in one of the corridors leading out of the hangar, waiting for the office to become vacant. He looked at the Doctor's directional detector, contemplating how best to render it useless.

The TARDIS was standing in a corner of the headmaster's office. Sarah, who had been making some preliminary notes about the appearances of the dinsoaurs, looked up as the Brigadier entered with General Finch and Sir Charles Grover.

"Where's the Doctor, Miss Smith?"

She nodded toward the open door of the TARDIS. "In there."

The Brigadier called into the police call box. "Doctor, could you spare us a moment?" Then he introduced Sarah to the Cabinet Minister.

The Doctor's head popped out of the TARDIS. "What is it now? I'm busy."

"The Minister has some information for you about this fellow Whitaker," explained the Brigadier.

The Doctor smiled. "Then you have my full attention."

"It's rather negative information," said Sir Charles. "I was chairman of the committee that considered Whitaker's application for a government grant. I actually saw his working papers. Not that I understood them, of course, but my scientific advisers assured me they were utter nonsense. All I can say is that the man is, or was, a harmless crank. He couldn't possibly be responsible for this dinosaur business."

Sarah spoke up, unable to contain herself. "That's not what I've heard, Sir Charles! I've spoken to his colleagues who were at Oxford with him, to the science correspondent of *The Times*, and to the editors of a number of scientific journals. They all say he was brilliant!"

Sir Charles turned to her with a kindly smile. "His work on the measurement of the internal weights of atoms was brilliant, Miss Smith, and so was his contribution to the analysis of magnectic infractions. But his ideas about Time travel were completely worthless." He turned back to the Doctor. "I understand you have set up an experiment that may give us a clue to the appearance of the dinosaurs? I'd be interested to hear more about it."

"I shall need the map of London to explain what I have in mind. Brigadier, may we all go to your office?" The Brigadier opened the door and ushered out the Doctor and Sir Charles. "General Finch, sir? Will you accompany us?"

"I have to get back to my own headquarters," said the General. He gazed at the police call box in silence until the Brigadier and the others had left. Then he spoke to Sarah. "You say this chap Whitaker disappeared, Miss Smith?"

"So far as I know. He vanished six months ago. Just upped and left home."

"A lot of people do disappear. They leave home, change their names, try to make new lives for themselves."

"Not famous scientists."

The General laughed gruffly. "A famous member of Parliament once tried to do it. We never know what pressures people are really undergoing."

"It seems to me," said Sarah, "that this is an enormous coincidence."

"What do you intend to do?"

"Keep looking for him," she replied with determination. "I'll make those pompous idiots believe me. Even the Brigadier's of no help. We've got that monster chained down, and he wouldn't let me take photographs of it—wouldn't even give me a pass to go back to the hangar."

"That seems most unfriendly of him," said the General, showing a softer side of his character. He took out a little notebook, wrote a few lines, and handed a slip of paper to her. "Take this to my Headquarters, see my Adjutant. He'll give you a pass."

Sarah was thrilled. "Thanks! Where is your HQ?"

70

"Show the note to my driver. He'll take you there."

Sarah was so pleased that she felt like giving the General a kis, but on second thought restrained herself. "Thank you, General. Thank you very much indeed." She rushed to the door, then paused. "What about you? Won't you need your car?"

"I have things to attend to here. Have a good trip."

"I will!" Sarah rushed out of the office, clutching the tiny slip of paper.

Alone, the General looked at the Doctor's workbench. After a few moments' search among the tools, he found the hacksaw that he was shortly going to need.

Sarah was studying the inert tyrannosaurus rex from the safety of the hangar office. She raised her miniature camera to take the first shot then remembered that the flashbulb would probably reflect against the glass window. She went through the door that led directly into the hangar.

Until now everything had happened so quickly she had scarcely had time to react to the situation. As she slowly circled the monster, she experienced a strange feeling of wonder and awe. She was examining a real living dinosaur, something that humans had never seen before because they had not developed until millions of years after the last of the giant dinosaurs had died. This animal lived—in a sense was still living—in a time when the world looked very different from today. Flowers did not exist in that world because insects had not yet evolved to carry pollen. To make life possible for so many varieties of cold-blooded reptiles, the atmosphere must have been warm and humid. The earliest mammals were just beginning to evolve, life forms that carried their babies within themselves instead of laying eggs.

She raised the camera to take the first photograph.

The flash apparatus flared for a split second, and in that split second the first photograph of a living dinosaur was recorded for all time. She took a series of photographs of the monster's bulk, then moved up to the enormous head. It was as she pressed the flash button for the fourth time that the tyrannosaurus's right eye blinked again.

The tyrannosaurus was suddenly, abruptly aware of blinding light. Programmed into its minuscule mind was intense fear of lightning storms. Being taller than most other animals, taller than much of the primeval foliage (there were very few trees then), the tyrannosaurus rex was a frequent victim of lightning strikes. And thunder and lightning were almost daily weather conditions in the warm balmy atmosphere of pre-history. Time and again the tyrannosaurus rex had seen its own kind killed outright when the daggers of electricity sliced down from the clouds.

With an ear-splitting roar, the monster raised its head, only to find its movements restricted by giant chains. Sarah raced back into the little hangar office, slamming the door. She went stright to the door that led to the corridor outside—and found it locked. She banged furiously on the door.

"Let me out! Who's locked this door?"

The tyrannosaurus rex tried moving its legs and its tail. All parts of itself were held down. Instinctively it struggled to become free. With a new strength born of fear and anger, it stretched out its legs until suddenly the chains snapped.

Sarah heard the crash of the giant chains as they slid from the monster's legs to the concrete floor. Unable to stop herself, she turned and watched in terror as the dinosaur now raised its neck, snapping the chains that held down the upper part of its body.

Temporarily exhausted by its efforts, the tyrannosaurus rex remained lying on the floor. Then it became aware of a noisy midget only a few yards away. Through the window it could see the midget with its mouth open, screaming. Most of the monster's prey was like this just before being eaten—mouth open in fear, making a loud noise. The thought triggered the sensation of hunger in the reptile's brain. It hadn't eaten since morning when it caught two very small dinosaurs. It moved its head forward to take a better look at its next meal.

Sarah beat her fists on the door to the corridor. "Help! Will someone open this door!"

There was no response. She felt sick with fear.

The tyrannosaurus rex moved its great snout forward to take its prey, and found its nose pressed against something that it couldn't see. This was bewildering. There was the prey, clearly visible, but some plate of invisible substance stood between them. It wriggled its great bulk round and started to bash at the little wooden office with its tail.

The first blow from the tail smashed the window. The second blow smashed in the entire window frame and fractured the wall. The third blow brought down part of the roof. A rafter hit Sarah's head, throwing her to the ground. The fourth blow was about to strike as the door to the corridor opened and the Doctor reached in, pulling Sarah to safety.

She was aware of being carried into the open air. She clung to the Doctor, weeping.

"It's all right, my dear," he said soothingly, "you're safe now."

Hearing a terrific crash of falling masonry, they looked up. The head of the giant tyrannosaurus rex was sticking up through the vast roof of the aircraft hangar.

"We must get away," shouted the Doctor. "If it does

73

give chase, I don't imagine it can outrun the speed of a jeep."

Sarah was bundled into the passenger seat. She turned back to look, fascinated and horrified, at the giant reptile.

"Doctor! It's vanishing!"

As they watched the tyrannosaurus rex dematerialized and was gone.

Sergeant Benton and two UNIT soldiers carefully laid the directional detector apparatus on the Doctor's work bench. The Doctor was busy inspecting the bump on Sarah's head which had been made by the falling rafter.

"The skin isn't broken," he told her, "but it will probably be a bit swollen for a day or two." He turned to the Brigadier. "The creature was still in the force field when it vanished, so perhaps the directional detector will tell us something."

Sergeant Benton carried in a couple of heavy sacks. "I think, Doctor, that what's in here might tell you something." He pulled from a bag a length of heavy chain. "Some of these links have been half-sawed through."

The Doctor took the chain from Benton. "By Jove, you're right!" He turned quickly to inspect the directional detector. "And this has been sabotaged. Not a single reading."

For a moment there was complete silence. The Brigadier dismissed the two UNIT privates, and turned to the Doctor. "So we have someone inside our organization working against us."

"Obviously." The Doctor rubbed his chin, thinking. "I shall now have to try a completely different approach."

74

"Are you going to catch another monster?" asked Sarah weakly.

"No," replied the Doctor, much to the relief of the Brigadier and Sergeant Benton. "We know these Time transferences must require enormous amounts of energy. I'm going to build a device that will detect that energy at its source."

"Why didn't you think of that in the first place?" asked the Brigadier, a little piqued. "Moving thirty tons of inert reptile from a cul-de-sac to that aircraft hangar was not my idea of fun!"

"Perhaps," said the Doctor disarmingly, "because even I cannot think of everything at once."

"Exactly how much energy would be needed to make those things appear, Doctor?" asked Sarah.

"Oh, you'd need something like a small nuclear generator."

"Then why don't we look for one?"

The Brigadier smiled self-importantly. "You may sometimes think we military chaps are stupid, Miss Smith, but that was one of the first things that occurred to me. I have made a thorough check and I can assure you there are no nuclear generators which have not been accounted for in the Central London area."

Sarah gave the Brigadier a savage look.

"I'm afraid the Brigadier's right," said the Doctor. "There can't be any nuclear generators around that nobody knows about. Why don't you try and get some rest? You had a nasty fright in that hangar."

"Thank you," said Sarah, apparently resigned. "I'll do that."

"Well," remarked the Doctor, "I'd better get started. Most of what I need is in the TARDIS. If you'll excuse me . . ." He produced his key, opened the door of the TARDIS, and went inside.

The Brigadier looked at his watch. "I'm due for yet another planning meeting with General Finch. Now he wants to hang looters in public! I sometimes think the poor fellow lives in a bygone age." He turned smartly and left the headmaster's office.

Sarah and Sergeant Benton were left facing each other. "Isn't it marvelous," she said scornfully. "I've just been told to go out and play!"

"The Doctor said you should get some rest."

"It comes to the same thing." She felt her temper rise. "They don't want to listen to me. Look, if there's a nuclear generator involved it must have been designed and assembled, and all that could be traced. There'd be records of it."

"The Brigadier's checked all that, miss," said Benton, loyally. "He found nothing."

"Maybe it was all secret," she said, thinking aloud.

The sergeant smiled. "Too secret for the Brigadier to know about?"

"Yes, why not?" Sarah had a sudden flash of inspiration. "Can you get me some transport?"

"I could try, miss. But where do you want to go?"

"Out to play," she replied pertly. "There can't be any harm in that, can there?"

"What a pleasant surprise," said Sir Charles Grover as he welcomed Sarah into his office. It was a small ministerial study, beautifully furnished, with a fine view of Big Ben and the Houses of Parliament. "I'm sorry you had to find your own way in here, but we're down to a skeleton staff. What can I do for you?"

"I'm very sorry to trouble you, Sir Charles." Sarah accepted his offer to sit down. "But you seem to be the only member of the Government still in London."

"Indeed I am." As he talked, he lit a little camping gas ring that had been set up on a corner table next to cups and saucers, a teapot, packet of tea, and a bottle of milk, all of which looked somewhat incongruous in a Cabinet Minister's office. "We have no catering staff now—nothing. But I *can* make you a cup of tea. Do you take milk and sugar?"

"Yes, please," she said. "One lump."

Sir Charles put a kettle onto the lit gas ring. "The rest of the Government shot off to Harrogate. But I said to the Prime Minister, 'If I'm in charge of the situation in London, I'm going to stay on the spot.' So here I am. How can I help you?"

Sarah quickly explained the Doctor's theory that it would require a nuclear generator to produce the vast amounts of power necessary for the Time transferences. She continued, "Wasn't there a plan once," she then asked, "to build underground quarters for the Government in the event of an atomic war breaking out?"

"That's true," said Sir Charles. "The Government of the day saw itself retreating to a hole in the ground where it would be safe." He laughed. "Goodness knows why! Just ten hydrogen bombs would have destroyed every city, every living person, every blade of grass in the British Isles. So they'd have had nothing to govern once the war was over!" He poured boiling water from the kettle into his teapot.

"Do you know whether any of these special underground shelters were ever built?" asked Sarah. "I remember reading about them. Weren't they all to have their own nuclear generators?"

"Now I see what you're getting at," Sir Charles said. "What a remarkable piece of thinking! But I don't think any of these places were ever built. I was only a junior back bencher in the House of Commons in those days. As far as I know, all the plans were shelved." He poured tea into two cups. "Have you talked about this to the Brigadier?"

"I'm not talking to anyone about it until I can get some evidence. I thought you might be able to help me."

Sir Charles stirred a cup of tea, lost in thought. "Maybe I can. There are Ministerial files here going back years, documents that I've never had time to study. Let's have a look." He crossed the study to a small door and opened it. "This is my filing room. Do come in."

Sarah entered the little windowless room. It was lined with gray metal filing cabinets. Sir Charles closed the door and pressed a button on the wall, causing a faint whirring sound.

"What's that?" she asked.

"The air conditioning." He opened one of the filing cabinet drawers and peered inside at a row of file tags. "I hardly understand the filing system myself. I've only been Minister six months, you know."

Sarah looked at a guide to the files on the wall. One item read *Top Secret Construction Projects.* "Could it be that one?" she asked.

"I wonder." He consulted the index. "That would be File 9941. Let's see if we can find it."

He walked along the row of filing cabinets. "We need the drawer whose files start with the number 9. Ah, here we are!" He pulled open the drawer, and after a moment's search found a manilla file numbered 9941.

Together they examined the contents of the file: letters, rough working papers of figures and costs, and a map. Sir Charles found a sealed envelope, quickly opened it, and glanced at the Ministerial letter it contained.

"Do you know, Miss Smith, you were right! They did build a fully equipped shelter for the Government to hide in. And—fancy that!—they never let the public know. Quite disgraceful."

But Sarah was staring at the map. "That must be Whitehall," she said, pointing. "And the exact position of the shelter would be . . ." She gasped.

Sir Charles's well-known politician's smile faded. His face set in stern lines. "That's right, Miss Smith. It was built, nuclear reactor and all, directly beneath this building. Shall we take a look at it?"

He gestured toward the door. Sarah turned, saw that the ornate carved door by which she had entered had been covered by a metal sliding door. The whirring sound stopped, and she felt the floor give a very slight bump. Sir Charles walked forward and pressed the button on the wall. The metal door slid to one side.

"This is my own very private elevator," said Sir Charles. "After you, Miss Smith."

Sarah stepped out into a metallic-walled corridor. A man wearing a white overall came toward them. A livid scar ran down one side of his face.

"We weren't expecting you, Sir Charles," said the man.

"Indeed not. This young lady is coming to stay with you for a while. Is everything going according to plan?"

The man nodded. "She is to be processed?"

"Immediately." Sir Charles turned to Sarah. "This man's name is Butler. He is a good man and will help you out of your dilemma."

"I'm not in a dilemma," she protested. "I want to be released immediately!"

"That isn't possible," said Sir Charles. "Come with me."

He walked ahead of her down the corridor, obviously very familiar with the place. Butler came up behind Sarah and occasionally hastened her along with a gentle shove. She followed Sir Charles.

Sir Charles opened a metal door that led into a small cell-like room. It contained one item of furniture—a

79

chair. "You will have to wait in here, Miss Smith. But no harm will come to you."

Butler pushed Sarah into the room.

"You're both mad!" she screamed.

"On the contrary," said Sir Charles, his well-known politician's smile starting to return now. "My associates and I are the only ones who are sane."

"Creating monsters in Central London is the work of lunatics."

"That is how it may seem to you. But there are very good reasons for it. When you understand everything you will be eternally grateful. Believe me, my dear, and try to trust me."

"They'll find me," she shouted. "You'll be sent to prison. The Doctor and the Brigadier will be searching for me!"

"I very much doubt it," said Sir Charles. "And certainly not where you're going."

Sir Charles nodded curtly and the Butler slammed the door.

Sarah paced angrily about the tiny room. How stupid to have walked straight into the trap! It was the same with that tyrannosaurus rex—she had brought it all on herself. The bump on her head was throbbing and she felt very fed up. She sat down on the chair and tried to stop herself from crying.

A light set in the metal wall opposite her started to blink on and off, red and green and orange. She moved the chair around to face a different wall. There another light was blinking, pink and blue and mauve. She moved the chair again, and found herself facing yet another light. And this time the light began to fascinate her. In a moment she was staring fixedly at the blinking light, and all the anger and fear drained from her mind.

6

The Spaceship

Sarah opened her eyes. A very handsome young man
was smiling down at her. His glinting fair hair was cut
short; his cheeks glowed with good health.

"Welcome to the people," he said gently.

"Who are you?"

"My name is Mark."

She turned her head to look about her. The walls and
ceiling made one huge curve—it was as though they
were inside a tube. She realized she was lying on her
back on a trolley.

"Where is this?"

"The spaceship," replied Mark. "You see it's all
come true."

Sarah struggled so sit upright. She looked down at
herself. She was wearing a very plain blue denim tunic.
Mark was similarly dressed.

"What's going on?" she asked, trying to conceal the
panic in her voice. "Where am I?"

Mark smiled again. "We left Earth three months ago.
Come and look."

With his help, Sarah got down from the trolley. Her
legs were unsteady, as though she had just awakened
from a very deep sleep. "This way," said Mark, leading
her to a porthole set in the curved wall. "Isn't that wonderful?"

Sarah looked through the porthole on to the black

81

vastness of Space. Distant suns showed as pin-pricks of light. "How did I get here?"

"You must have forgotten. It's understandable. But the Elders will explain everything. Let's go and meet them. Come."

He held out his hand. Cautiously Sarah took it, and allowed herself to be led through a curved metal corridor. They entered a large communal area with many portholes, tables, and chairs. A middle-aged man with white hair and a white goatee beard was seated at a table carving a wooden bowl. Close by, a tall, rather beautiful gray-haired woman was making cloth on a treadle weaving machine. Both wore blue denim tunics.

"Here she is!" Mark announced.

The man and woman looked up and smiled. The woman left her weaving and came over to embrace Sarah.

"You're the first to recover," she said, kissing Sarah lightly on the cheek. "Welcome back to the people."

Sarah pulled away from the woman. "Who are you?"

The white-haired man came over to her and extended his hand. "My name is Adam. This is Ruth."

Sarah looked at them in astonishment. "Surely those aren't your real names!" She turned to the woman. "I interviewed you about that Bill of yours in the House of Lords against the pollution of rivers." She pointed to the man. "And you're Nigel Castle, the novelist."

"Not any more," said the man who liked to be called Adam. "Now I work with my hands."

Sarah turned back to look more closely at the young man called Mark. "And now I remember you, too. You're John Crichton. You ran the three-minute mile. What are you all doing here?"

"The same as you, my dear," said Ruth. "We are on our way to New Earth, a small planet similar to Earth but at an earlier stage of development."

"You've been in suspended animation for three months," Adam informed her. "But it will all come back to you when you fully recover. New Earth is still pure, undefiled by the evil of Man's technology. There is air that is still clean to breathe, and a simple pastoral people, innocent and unspoiled. It will be our task to guide them so that the evils developed on Earth shall not be repeated."

Sarah was convinced these people were mad. She decided to humor them. "Just the four of us have to do all that?"

Mark laughed. "You really are forgetting things. There are over two hundred of us on this ship. Look." He crossed to a monitor screen set in the wall and pressed a button. The screen lit up showing the interior of another compartment in the spaceship. Tiers of bunks lined the walls, each carrying a sleeping person. "We have six slumber chambers," he said. "They'll all be recovering soon, just as you did."

"And this is only one of the ships in the fleet," said Adam, beaming. "It's a whole armada of people who wish to take intelligence and right-thinking to New Earth."

Sarah asked, "Why are all those people asleep?"

"To save food and oxygen," Ruth explained. "It's a three-month journey, remember. And now almost over."

"You mean to say I've been here three months?" said Sarah. "I can't believe it."

Bewildered, Sarah ran her fingers through her hair. Her forefinger touched the bump on her head. It was still very tender. At that moment she knew she could only have been on the spaceship for a few hours.

Ruth said, "Is something wrong?"

Sarah smiled. "No, of course not. It's all very excit-

83

ing. And now I'm just starting to get my memory back."

The Doctor roared down Whitehall on a big Army motorcycle which had been lent to him by the Brigadier. A motorcycle, he explained to the Brigadier, was the quickest way to get around London, and he had to cover a large area in the shortest possible time. Strapped to the handlebars was the energy detecting device he had built, a compact black box with a simple on-off control, and a dial that registered the presence of high-voltage electricity. He had already covered two sections of London, duly marked off on the map in his pocket. A few minutes ago, as he turned into Trafalgar Square, the needle on the detector's dial flickered for the first time. As he drove around Trafalgar Square at high speed, he found the needle flickered most actively when he was close to the opening to Whitehall.

He arrived in Parliament Square, deserted except for a few pigeons. The needle registered to the number 4 on the detector dial. Slowly the Doctor drove round the empty square. Going toward Victoria Street, the reading dropped to 3; completing the circuit of the square and heading back toward Westminster Bridge, the needle jumped to 5. He stopped the motorcycle outside Westminster Underground Station, unfastened the detector from the handlebars, and carried it to the metal gates that barred the entrance to the station. The needle moved to 5.02. The Doctor found his set of skeleton keys in his capacious pockets and opened the gates. He went down the dirty, unswept steps of the station.

Inside, the station was in complete darkness. The Doctor fished out his torch and continued down the steps to one of the platforms. The dial now read 5.08. Cautiously the Doctor moved along the railway platform. He stopped to listen. There was a faint humming

84

sound. Swinging his torch round to the wall, the Doctor saw a metal airvent grille. He went over, bent down and listened. He could just hear the distant hum of a machine, probably an air-ventilation plant. He plucked out his large silk handkerchief, and held it in front of the vent between finger and thumb. The handkerchief was sucked *toward* the vent by a slight air flow. How very, very odd! The airvents in London underground stations pump air *into* the stations; this one was sucking air *away* from the station. So someone, somewhere must be needing a constant supply of air.

Footsteps. Someone was coming down the stairs to the platform. The Doctor slid full-length under one of the bench-type seats that jutted from the wall, and extinguished his torch. The footsteps came nearer, and now the glare of a torch carried by someone in a hurry. Looking up from his hiding place, the Doctor could just discern the outline of a man in the spill of light from the man's torch. The man stopped by a louvred door set in the wall. He did something to the door that the Doctor couldn't see; immediately there was the sound of an elevator ascending. Fifteen seconds later light glared through the louvres of the door as the elevator came up and stopped. The Doctor risked his luck and craned his neck out from under the bench. As the man opened the door the Doctor caught a glimpse of a livid scar running down his cheek. The man, dressed in a lounge suit and carrying a large suitcase, entered the elevator. A moment later its glaring light sank down and out of sight.

The Doctor crawled out from under the bench and brushed down his clothes. He listened until the noise of the elevator machinery stopped. Then he shone his torch on the louvred door and inspected it closely. There was no keyhole. He tried to guess what the man had done to activate the elevator, and ran his fingers down the slats. The fifth slat turned on an axis. Instantly, the elevator machinery came to life. Fifteen seconds later, light glared through the louvres. The elevator door opened with ease, to reveal a cleaners' cupboard containing mops and pails. He stepped inside, and pulled the door shut. Then he searched for a control that would activate the elevator from inside. There was nothing to be seen except two hooks in the wall. From one of them hung a cleaner's overall. The Doctor touched the empty hook, and found that it could be maneuvred like a little lever. He turned it round on its in-built axis until it pointed straight down. The elevator started to descend.

Butler opened the suitcase to let Professor Whitaker examine its contents. "Do you now have *everything* you need, Professor?"

Whitaker picked over the electronic equipment that filled the suitcase. "I don't know yet. If I need anything more, you'll have to provide it."

"It isn't easy getting this stuff for you. Every time I go out in the streets I risk being shot as a looter."

Professor Whitaker stepped back from the open suitcase. "If you're going to make a big *thing* of it, let's forget the entire project!"

Butler would very much have liked to batter Professor Whitaker's head to pulp. He smiled and said, "You will have your little joke, Professor. Don't take me seriously."

But Whitaker was sulking. "I know when I'm not welcome. If it's *such* a problem to provide me with the equipment that's vital for Operation Golden Age, you only have to say."

Twice when Butler was entering electronic shops in the Tottenham Court Road and Lisle Street to take these things for Whitaker, he had had to hide like a thief from Army patrols. He hated these trips outside because of their danger; even more, he hated being cooped up with this peculiar professor day and night under the ground. "I am very sorry for what I just said, Professor. Will you be kind enough to accept my sincere and most abject apologies?"

Professor Whitaker regarded him for half a minute. Then the flicker of a smile. "You really are sorry?"

"Yes." said Butler, wishing he could drive his fist into Whitaker's pale face and break all his teeth, "I really am terribly sorry. Obviously you must have all the equipment that you need for the great experiment which only you can carry out."

"All right," said Whitaker, coming back to the suitcase, "let's have a proper look at what you've got for me."

Butler lifted out a piece of electronic equipment. "You said you wanted one of these."

Whitaker clapped his hands with delight. "A thermal dynometer! How terribly clever of you to get one—"

He stopped short. Something had caught his eye. The elevator indicator was flashing. "It seems we are going to have company," he said.

Butler rushed to one of the TV monitors and pressed a button. On to the screen flashed a picture of the corridor by the elevators. One of the elevator doors opened and the Doctor stepped out.

"Who on earth is that?" said Professor Whitaker.

Butler's face looked grim. "The Doctor, UNIT's scientific adviser. I'll kill him."

"You'll do no such thing," Whitaker protested. He looked keenly at the Doctor, who was now peering up and down the corridor wondering which way to go. "He's terribly handsome."

"What do you want me to do?"

"Oh, play games with him," said Whitaker. "You know what to do. Just send him away."

Whitaker returned to the suitcase. Butler knew it might only annoy Whitaker again if he didn't carry out the order, and his strict instructions were to keep the Professor happy at all costs. He crossed to the panel of controls that activated the control center's radiation-proof internal doors.

The Doctor glanced up and down the corridor. He caught sight of a large notice on the wall with daggers pointing in different directions. It read:

CABINET ROOM
PRIME MINISTER'S DAY ROOM
SECRETARIAT
ROYAL SUITE
KENNELS
SLEEPING QUARTERS
VICTUALS
SICK BAY
COMMUNICATIONS ROOM
NUCLEAR REACTOR

The Doctor hurried off in the direction indicated for the nuclear reactor. He found himself in a labyrinth of corridors. At each intersection signs indicated the way to different Government departments. He realized that this place was to have been the British seat of government had atomic war broken out. He turned into yet another corridor; at the far end was a door bearing the words NUCLEAR REACTORS—KEEPOUT. He raced toward the door. A heavy metal shutter slammed down in front of him, completely blocking his way. On it were the words RADIATION SHUTTER. Now he knew that his presence had been detected. He turned around and raced back up the corridor and turned a corner. Another shutter fell from its slot in the ceiling, barring his way.

He made off in another direction. More shutters came down before him. He noticed that at some points, where shutter slits were clearly visible in the ceiling, the shutters did not come down. So they were playing a game with him, guiding him, by closing up some corridors, in the direction that they wanted him to go.

Finally he found himself back at the corridor outside the elevator. The elevator door stood open invitingly. At either end of the corridor shutters came down. He got into the elevator among the mops and pales and brooms, and turned the clothes hook to point upward. The door closed and the elevator started to ascend. He hadn't found everything he wanted, but he had seen enough. As the elevator neared the Underground Station, it crossed his mind that they could have killed him but had let him escape alive. He wondered why.

Butler turned to Professor Whitaker. "I've guided him back to the elevator. He'll go and tell everyone what he's seen." He felt he was not getting the Professor's full attention. Whitaker was concentrating on something he was doing at the Timescoop. "I said he's escaping," said Butler. "Remember, you didn't want me to kill him. Do you realize what will happen now?"

Professor Whitaker replied, "I've changed my mind. Come and look."

Butler crossed to the Timescoop. Above the main console of controls was a small television monitor screen. On the screen a large pterodactyl in a sandy barren landscape was sitting on a rock.

"Just think," said Whitaker. "That ghastly looking creature is actually sitting on that rock at this very moment."

"But millions of years ago."

"Don't be so argumentative. All right, it *was* sitting exactly like that, and I've tuned in to it."

"Most impressive," replied Butler distractedly. He was wondering how he could make his escape before the Brigadier and goodness knew who else descended to arrest them all. "But the Doctor is still escaping. We are in a very serious situation, Professor Whitaker."

"You don't think I've summoned up that awful-looking pterodactyl just for fun, do you? Now watch." He adjusted two master controls. The pterodactyl became transparent, then vanished.

"Where have you sent it?"

Professor Whitaker giggled. "Guess!"

The elevator came to a stop. The Doctor pushed open the louvred door, switched on his torch, and stepped on to the platform of the Underground Station. He strode purposefully off down the corridor, his head buzzing with his discoveries, toward the steps that led up to street level. He stopped. What was that noise? Swinging up the torch he caught a swooping pterodactyl in the beam. He flung himself to one side as it flapped by, the tip of one leathery wing grazing his cheek. The Doctor trained the torch on the flying reptile as it wheeled round to attack again. He dived full-length at the platform—but the bird anticipated its prey's move by back-flapping in full flight, and landed by the Doctor's head, huge jaws open to tear at the flesh of the Doctor's face! The Doctor swung the torch round and shone it full into the monster's eyes. Screeching loudly, the pterodactyl flew up to the roof of the station. The Doctor scrambled to his feet and raced down the station, the flapping wings pursuing him. At the opening to the stairs the pterodactyl found its wing span too great to go through. The Doctor escaped up the stairs. Being now in total darkness, the pterodactyl settled down to wait for sunrise.

The Reminder Room

Sarah looked through the glass door that led to the flight deck. The one seat which faced the console of instruments was empty. From time to time, the levers on the console moved of their own accord.

"Why is there no pilot?"

"It's not necessary," replied Mark, who was showing Sarah around the spaceship. "The controls are all on automatic pilot, locked to the controls of the leading ship."

"Extraordinary." She extended her hand to open the glass door.

Mark showed alarm. "You mustn't go in there!"

Sarah quickly withdrew her hand. "Why not?"

"None of us can go in there. The controls are very delicate. When we arrive, the ship will land automatically." He smiled. "And our Golden Age will begin."

Sarah screwed up her face, and pretended that she couldn't remember what he meant. "My memory still isn't very good, Mark. How will we live?"

"We shall found a settlement. We have seed, tools, and enough provisions to keep us going for a year. We'll be like the Pilgrim Fathers who went to America."

"What about the present inhabitants of the planet? I don't think the Red Indians liked the Pilgrim Fathers very much. Maybe these people won't like us."

"We shall treat them kindly and decently," Mark in-sisted. "We'll guide them, and make sure they don't make the same mistakes that were made on Earth."

"What mistakes?"

"Surely you know. Factories and mines that destroy the landscape. Explosives of all kinds that kill and maim. Cars and airplanes that pollute the atmosphere."

Ruth and Adam appeared from the direction of the main living quarters. "Finding it interesting?" Adam asked Sarah.

"Very. Mark's just reminding me about all the awful things humans have done to ruin Earth." She turned back to the young athlete. "But what about medicine and education? Surely they were *good* things."

Ruth laughed. "Compared with its evils, the benefits of technological civilization are very few."

Adam took up the argument. "Supermarkets, color television, plastic cups. But what are they all worth?"

"They make life comfortable for a lot of people."

Adam, ignoring Sarah's reply, continued: "We shall take the good, but leave the evil behind."

"And who decides which is which?"

"It's all so obvious." Adam's eyes began to look like those of a prophet who was in personal communication with God.

"But don't you think that people have a right to choose the kind of life they want?" Sarah blurted out.

Ruth looked at her a little sternly. "People on Earth were allowed to choose—and see what kind of a world they made! Moral degradation, permissiveness, cheating, lying, cruelty!"

Ruth's one-sided attitude angered Sarah. "There is also a lot of love and kindness and honesty! Didn't you ever notice those things on Earth?"

Ruth's mouth set into hard lines. "You mustn't say such things!"

Mark grinned. "I'm sure Sarah meant nothing—"

92

"Oh yes I did!" interrupted Sarah. "And I'll say whatever I like. I've met people like your lot before. Everything you believe in must be absolutely right! If anyone dares to disagree with you, you don't even listen!"

Adam turned to Ruth. He spoke as though Sarah wasn't even present. "I was assured by the organizers that everyone had been carefully selected and screened."

"You see! You even talk to each other as if I didn't exist!"

"We have to consider the good of the majority," Adam snapped. "I don't think you're going to be very happy with us. If you are not of a like mind, why did you choose to join us?"

"I didn't! I was brought here against my wishes."

"Impossible. Quite impossible. The re-awakening must have affected your mind."

"I quite agree," added Ruth. "She'll have to go to the Reminder Room."

Sarah backed away. "What's that?"

Adam gripped her arm firmly. "You are in desperate need of re-education."

"Don't worry, child," said Ruth, taking Sarah's other arm. "Very soon you will have returned to our point of view—about everything."

The Brigadier's jeep stopped outside Westminister Underground Station, followed by the two other UNIT jeeps.

"Two men stand guard by the vehicles," called the Brigadier. "The rest of us will follow you, Doctor."

The UNIT soldiers opened the gates. The Doctor ran down the steps into the underground station, the boots of UNIT soldiers clattering behind him.

"What I can't understand," shouted the Brigadier,

running to keep up with the Doctor, "is why they let you escape."

"They tried to kill me by materializing a pterodactyl. I'm fortunate to be alive."

"They had reached the platform now. The Doctor raced toward the cubicle which had contained the mops and pails, and wrenched open the door. "This is the elevator. And this is how you work it . . ."

His voice trailed off. The hooks had disappeared.

"Something wrong?" asked the Brigadier.

"There's an airvent on the platform," said the Doctor, stepping backward out of the cubicle. "Let's check that."

The Doctor pulled out his large silk handkerchief and hung it from finger and thumb in front of the airvent. There was no movement of air at all.

"It looks," said the Brigadier, "as though the birds have flown." He thought of a feeble joke. "Along with their pterodactyls."

The Doctor straightened up, pocketing his handkerchief. "Don't you believe me about this place?"

"Of course I do," answered the Brigadier. "Have you ever known me not to believe you, Doctor? But it looks as though there is now no proof. And no way into that control center you told me about!"

Sir Charles Grover listened attentively to his visitor's report about the underground control center. When the Doctor had finished, Grover smiled. "You must have been talking to Miss Smith, Doctor."

The Doctor was puzzled by the reply. "What do you mean?"

"She came here with a most marvelous theory that such a place had once been built right under Central London."

"She came to see *you*?" queried the Brigadier.

94

"She thought I might know about it," replied Grover honestly. "We checked the files together. Why look, I still have the file on my desk!" Grover picked up a manilla folder and opened it. "See for yourself, Doctor. This explains the entire plan for an underground seat of government in the event of atomic war." He handed the file to the Doctor. "You will also see a memorandum stating that the idea was later abandoned and the place never constructed." Grover had typed the memo himself fifteen minutes before the arrival of the Doctor and the Brigadier.

The Doctor glanced briefly at the contents of the folder. "You will forgive me, Minister, but I prefer to believe the evidence of my own eyes. Where did Miss Smith go after she visited you?"

"Back to UNIT."

"Are you sure of that, sir?" asked the Brigadier. "We haven't seen her for some time."

Grover pretended to rack his brains. "She turned up here in a UNIT car. I sent that straight back because I didn't want to keep your driver waiting. Then, after we'd had our little chat, I sent her back to you in my own ministerial car."

The Brigadier looked puzzled. "She didn't arrive. Perhaps she asked your driver to take her somewhere else?"

"I could check that for you." Grover lifted his internal phone and spoke into it. "Will you send in my chauffeur, please?" He put down the phone, and turned back to the Doctor and the Brigadier. "A cup of tea, gentlemen? With no catering staff in London, I have this little gadget over here for brewing up. Would you care for some?"

"It's very kind," said the Doctor. But not just now, thank you." He paused. "Sir Charles, I have definitely

95

been into an underground place that was humming with life, and it can't be very far from here."

Grover smiled at the Doctor, as one might to a madman. "I'm sure you *believe* you've been in such a place, Doctor. But since you now admit that you can't find your way in again . . ."

A tap on the door. A uniformed chauffeur entered and stood to attention. Grover turned to the man.

"Where did you take the young lady who was visiting me?"

The man in chauffeur's uniform answered, "Back to UNIT Headquarters, sir."

"You're quite sure of that?"

"Yes, sir. I saw her go inside."

"Right, that will be all, thank you."

As the chauffeur turned to go, the Doctor noticed a livid scar that ran down the man's left cheek.

The Reminder Room made Sarah think of the little cell where she had been hypnotized by the flashing lights. Small and windowless, it, too, contained a single chair, but this one was bolted to the middle of the floor. The chair faced a screen that filled the whole of one wall. After she had been locked in the room for a few minutes a film started to play on the screen, obviously specially made to "remind" any doubting members that they had been right to join the group. All the shots were of bad things on Earth: mounds of wrecked cars, factory chimneys belching black smoke, oil on beaches, dead fish in polluted rivers, traffic jams, jet planes roaring over crowded cities. A commentator's voice boomed from loudspeakers set in the four corners of the little room.

"Ever since the Industrial Revolution, Man has polluted his planet, until now his only home. Not only has Man ruined his own environment, he has made life impossible for other living creatures. Seventy-five species of animals were made extinct in the first seventy-five years of this century. Others are threatened. The Giant Lemurs of Madagascar may soon suffer the same fate as the King Kangaroos of Australia—"

The film and the commentary stopped abruptly. The door opened and Mark came in. He was carrying a tray containing a glass of water and a piece of brown bread.

"I've brought you something to eat."

Sarah looked at the bread and water. "No chance of my getting overweight."

"The bread is pure. This diet will help cleanse your body of toxic things; and that will help to clear your mind."

"Very thoughtful of you. In olden times witches were burnt to death to save their souls."

"We're not like that," Mark smiled, not taking Sarah seriously. "We only want to help you."

"That's what they always said to the witches." She started to eat the bread; it was awful. "Why won't you believe that I was kidnapped and put on this ship?"

"Because that's impossible. Now watch the film. It will remind you of the truth."

Before Sarah could stop him, he left, locking the door behind him. Immediately the film came back on the screen. It showed a traffic policeman in Tokyo.

". . . after two hours controlling traffic, this policeman must be given one full hour of oxygen treatment. So much for the pleasure of motoring . . ."

The film continued. Sarah munched her piece of bread.

Sir Charles Grover was presiding over the planning meeting in the Cabinet Room of the underground control center. Portraits of Disraeli, Gladstone, Churchill, and President Kennedy hung from the oak-paneled walls of the windowless room. Seated round a huge table covered in expensive red leather were Professor Whitaker, General Finch and Captain Michael Yates.

Whitaker spoke up. "Final tests have all been positive. When the power build-up from the reactor is complete we shall be ready for the final countdown."

"How much longer to wait?" growled General Finch.

Whitaker waved his hand. "Only a few hours, General. You must learn patience."

Finch turned away. He couldn't stand the sight of Whitaker. "I hope you realize that they're trying to trace our learned Professor," he said to Grover.

"Don't forget, General, that they've also discovered this place—thanks to you people!" said Whitaker. "Why could you not guarantee a little peace and security for my work? It's frightful having this Doctor person prowling around."

"I told you not to underestimate the Doctor," said Yates.

"We ought to dispose of him," snapped General Finch.

"If we do that," replied the Captain, "we shall not be worthy of our cause."

"Quite right," agreed Grover placatingly. "We must maintain our high ideals. Under no circumstances shall we descend to murder."

"Then what do we do about the Doctor?" asked General Finch.

Grover smiled. "We shall discredit him."

While the instigators of Operation Golden Age conferred deep in the bowels of Central London, the Brigadier and the Doctor were talking in the Doctor's workshop at UNIT Headquarters.

"I always try to believe you, Doctor, but there isn't a scrap of evidence that this underground place exists. Sir

98

Charles Grover showed us the memo that confirmed it had never been built."

"He's implicated. Don't you realize that?"

The Brigadier laughed. "Why should the Minister be involved in the apparition of monsters?"

"The reptiles are a side issue. They are a device to clear Central London, that's all. Something much bigger is under way. You must go back to that underground station with explosives and blast your way in."

The Brigadier was taken aback. "That's public property! I'd need permission from General Finch before I could start blowing up underground stations!"

"Then get it!"

"All right," said the Brigadier with a shrug, "I'll try."

He hurried out. The Doctor began searching for paper on which to write a full report of the dinosaur apparitions for the government in Harrogate. Suddenly, Sergeant Benton burst in.

"Doctor, there's a phone call for you. It came through on the UNIT line, but you can take it in here."

"Thank you." The Doctor picked up the headmaster's phone. "Hello?"

"My name is Whitaker. I understand that you've been trying to trace me."

"I have indeed. Are you behind these dinosaur appearances?"

"In a way, but I was tricked. I've escaped and now they're after me."

"Who's after you?"

There was a pause. "I don't want to talk over the phone. Can we meet?"

"Where are you?"

"In the aircraft hangar where you were conducting your experiments. I hoped you might still be there."

"I'll get over there as quickly as possible." The Doctor cradled the receiver, and bolted through the door.

The Doctor dismounted from his Army motorcycle, and ran into the vast building. All the soldiers had been dismissed after the disappearance of the tyrannosaurus. He walked through deserted corridors calling Professor Whitaker's name. No response. He continued toward what remained of the little office inside the huge hangar. It was just as he and Sarah had left it—the window and its frame destroyed, the wall crumbling, part of the ceiling fallen in. What he didn't notice among the wreckage was the miniature television eye that was watching him. A stray cat mewed. The Doctor turned. The cat was climbing up over the wreckage, sniffing about for food. All at once the cat started to walk backward, exactly retracing its steps. The Doctor realized he was in the center of a localized Time eddy. He peered through the gaping hole that had been the window into the hangar. A fully grown stegosaurus was beginning to appear and already he could hear its heavy breathing.

"Professor Whitaker," he shouted, "did you just bring me here to show how clever you are? I already know you can materialize things from the past. So come out of hiding and let's talk."

The door behind him burst open. General Finch and a group of soldiers entered, the Brigadier following.

"There's your monster-maker," barked the General. "Caught in the act!"

The Brigadier stepped forward. "Doctor, you are under arrest."

8

Escape!

". . . Greed and aggression lead to the greatest crime of all—war. With the hydrogen bomb Man now has the choice of destroying his planet quickly through war or slowly through pollution . . ."

In the Reminder Room, the voice of the film's commentator droned on. Sarah knew that everything the voice said was true. What she didn't agree with was the way in which these people on the spaceship were trying to run away from the problem, and their schoolmasterly attitude toward anyone who thought differently. Suddenly the film and the voice stopped. The door opened and Mark looked in.

"How are you feeling now?"

"Hungry, tired, and I've got a headache."

"Is the film helping you?"

"Can't you ever understand? You're here because you want to be. I'm a kidnapped prisoner."

He frowned. "You will have to drop this ridiculous story, Sarah."

"Why? It's the truth."

He looked around to make sure no one was listening in the corridor, then quietly closed the door behind him. "The elders, Adam and Ruth, are not going to permit a disruptive influence among us."

"Do you mean they're going to kill me?" She tried to hide the fear in her voice. "Is that what they'll do?"

101

He averted his eyes. "They are really sweet, gentle people. They are both vegetarians because animals have to die to provide humans with meat. But they are determined that nothing shall go wrong with our great mission."

Sarah thought about this. A veteran journalist once told her, "Beware people who *know* they are right, like Oliver Cromwell. For the good of Humanity, those people sometimes do murder." She decided to act up to Mark. "Perhaps the time in suspended-animation affected my thinking. I don't even remember how I came to be here. Tell me about it."

He smiled, overjoyed that Sarah was no longer persisting with her stupid kidnapping story. "There were just a few of us at first," he said enthusiastically. "We all shared a disgust with the way life was going on Earth. At first there seemed nothing we could do. Then one of our members, an astronomer, told us of this planet that we call New Earth. And another of us, a scientist, invented the space-drive that would take us there. We all contributed money to help build the fleet of spaceships."

"Did we *see* the spaceships?"

"Of course not. They were built secretly. Don't you remember how you were hypnotized before coming on board?"

"Yes," she replied with complete honesty. "I remember that part very well."

"We had to report to that special place in the center of London, and then each in turn was hypnotized into suspended-animation—so's to save oxygen and food on the three-month journey."

"Of course," she pretended to remember. "It's all coming back now. But I can't recall how I first heard about the scheme?"

"The organizers advertised in newspapers and magazines." Mark grinned. "Naturally they didn't announce what it was *really* all about! They were small advertisements, seeking people who might be interested in setting up a commune and starting a new life. Thousands and thousands of people replied."

"I bet they did. Mark, you've made it all clear to me now. Will you take me to the elders so that I can tell them that I now remember correctly?"

"I'd be delighted."

He held the door open wide. Sarah dashed into the corridor, pulled the door shut behind her, and bolted it.

"Sorry about that," she called through the closed door. "Enjoy the movie."

As she hurried down the corridor she heard Mark pounding on the closed door behind her.

The Doctor was led, handcuffed, into the classroom at UNIT's Headquarters. Two armed soldiers marched on either side of him, followed by Captain Yates, General Finch, and the Brigadier.

"So that's the end of that," barked General Finch. "Take those handcuffs off him, and put him into a cell."

"With respect, sir," said the Brigadier, as one of the soldiers removed the Doctor's handcuffs, "we have no cells here."

"Then lock him up in one of the rooms. Make sure he doesn't escape. The man is dangerous and possibly mad."

"Shouldn't we question him?" said the Brigadier.

"There's no need. I shall send a report to the Government immediately to say that we have arrested the monster-maker."

"Once I'm under lock and key," the Doctor chipped in, "you can bring back those millions of Londoners."

"That's a point, sir," said the Brigadier. "If the crisis is over, shouldn't we end the evacuation?"

The General looked uncertain. "All in good time, Brigadier. There are many complicated arrangements to be made first. Until you receive further instructions, keep this maniac under close arrest. He is not to make contact with anyone. Captain Yates is to remain in charge of the prisoner. The Brigadier is to come with me. There is much to be done."

The General turned on his heel and marched out of the classroom, the Brigadier following obediently. The Doctor was delighted to find himself alone with Captain Yates. The two UNIT soldiers remained well in the background.

"Listen, Mike," the Doctor whispered urgently, "there isn't much time. I need all the men you can muster and some high explosives to break into their control center before the final phase of their plan . . ."

To the Doctor's astonishment, Captain Yates wasn't paying any attention. Instead, he opened the door and called, "Sergeant Benton, in here please!"

The Doctor touched Yates's arm. "Are you on their side as well, Mike?" For years the Doctor and Captain Yates had been good friends.

Yates would not turn to face the Doctor. "I'm sorry," he muttered quietly. "What we are doing is for the good of Humanity. I know that what we are doing is right."

Sergeant Benton hurried into the classroom. "Sir?"

"The Doctor is under arrest," said Captain Yates. "Keep him under constant guard. Find somewhere to lock him up. I'll leave you to it." Without looking at the Doctor, Captain Yates quickly left the classroom.

Benton couldn't believe what he had just been told. "You are under arrest, Doctor?"

"That's right. Where are you going to keep me prisoner?"

Benton paused to think, and then he addressed the

two UNIT soldiers. "You two, go and fix up the text-book store room as a temporary cell." The two soldiers looked apprehensive at leaving the Doctor, now regarded as a dangerous criminal, alone with the unarmed sergeant. He shouted at them, "Jump to it!" The soldiers hurried out of the classroom. Benton turned back to the Doctor, lowering his voice, "Now tell me the truth, Doctor, what's going on?" He had known the Doctor some years and trusted him implicitly.

"I'm still not entirely sure, but General Finch is mixed up in it, and Captain Yates, too."

Benton's eyes widened. "Captain Yates?!"

"They've won him over somehow," said the Doctor. "He's a good man, and believes what they are doing is good in some way."

"Strewth! There's only one thing for it—you'll have to knock me out!" Benton stood to attention and closed his eyes. "Use your Venusian karate to overpower me, so that I'll be lying here unconscious when the soldiers get back."

"Thank you. I promise not to hurt you." He gently applied the Venusian karate hold with two fingers to Benton's neck. Benton lost consciousness almost immediately. The Doctor carefully lowered him to the floor.

"Thanks again," said the Doctor, looking down at the prostrate form of Benton. He hurried out through the door.

". . . Man is the only animal to prey on his own species. As society breaks down, armed gangsters take over. In America, with fifty murders a day, law-abiding citizens live behind electrified fences to keep criminals out. In the City of London another type of criminal exists. Property developers have destroyed—"

The film and its commentary stopped automatically

105

as Sarah opened the door of the Reminder Room. Mark, more concerned for Sarah's safety than angry, swung around to greet her.

"Sarah, you could put yourself in great danger by escaping like that. The elders would be furious! Where have you been?"

She stepped into the room and closed the door. "You've got to listen to me, Mark. I've been looking around this spaceship. There's something you must see with your own eyes. This isn't a real spaceship at all."

He took a step back from her, as one might retreat from a raving lunatic. "You told me your memory was returning . . ."

"I was lying, to put you at ease, so that I could escape from this stupid Reminder Room." She opened the door. "Follow me. I'm going to show you something."

"No, you must stay in here. The film will help you get back your sanity."

Sarah realized she could not make Mark follow her by force. She had to win him over through argument. "I'll make a deal with you. I want you to see something that will help *your* sanity, and you want me to see the rest of this film. I've already seen part of it. Isn't it my turn to show *you* something? Then, if you're not convinced, I'll come back here and see the rest of the film."

He thought about that. "All right, but no tricks. And don't try to escape."

"If this is a real spaceship, Mark, I *can't* escape, can I? Now come on."

He followed her down the corridor to the main living area of the spaceship. It was deserted. She crossed to the glass door of the flight deck. The unmanned controls were still moving in apparent response to the automatic pilot apparatus.

"Come in here." She opened the door to the flight deck.

Mark held back. "We are under express orders never to enter the flight deck."

"Of course, because there's something they don't want you to know. Forget your silly orders and follow me."

He went inside with her. Through the for'ard portholes they could see the infinite black vista of Space, studded with distant suns. Sarah put her hands under the outer edge of the control console and lifted it.

"You'll damage it!" Mark yelled.

"No I won't. There isn't anything to damage. Look."

Mark looked into the cavity which Sarah had revealed beneath the control console. There was nothing there except a small electric motor that made the levers on the control console move. "You see," she said, "it's all a fake."

"There must be some explanation," he said lamely.

Sarah let the panel drop back into position. "Mark, where exactly is this planet we're heading for?"

"The organizers said it was in another solar system, close to Earth."

"The nearest possible solar system to Earth is four light years away. If we traveled in the most advanced spaceships developed on Earth, it would take hundreds of years to reach there."

"But one of our members invented a new space drive."

"You're not a scientist, Mark. You would have believed anything." Sarah parted her hair to reveal the bump on her head. "See that? I got it just before I was kidnapped. If I'd been on this so-called spaceship three months, it would have gone down by now."

Mark looked confused. "I don't know what to think. If we aren't on a spaceship, where are we?"

"I think this is a dummy. It's the sort of thing big

107

stores build in their toy departments at Christmas for the kiddies."

"That's ridiculous!"

"Then I'll prove it to you." She walked toward the door at the end of the flight deck. Across it ran the words KEEP SHUT WHEN IN SPACE. She put her hand on the lever. "I'm going out through this hatch."

"It opens directly into Space! You'll be killed. All the oxygen will rush out of the ship," cried Mark desperately. "We'll all be killed."

"The flight deck is supposedly airtight," she explained. "So go back through that glass door, close it, and watch me from a position of safety."

Mark moved forward to grab Sarah. "No! I won't let you!"

She started to pull the lever. "You can't stop me. Once I pull this lever we'll both be sucked out into a vacuum, if we're really in Space. Get back. I'm going to pull the lever."

Mark backed away reluctantly, and passed the open door to the main living quarters. Then he closed the glass-paneled door and watched.

Sarah turned her back on him. She didn't want him to see her close her eyes and pray as she yanked back the lever. If they really were in Space, the moment the hatch opened all the air would leave her lungs. Her lifeless young body would float away into a black nothingness, lost forever.

Corporal Bryson had the classroom to himself. He idly glanced at the map of London which covered the blackboard. Were people really seeing things? He counted the flags. But how could so many people be wrong? He sat down in the Brigadier's comfortable chair, put his booted feet on the desk, and opened the comic that he always carried in his tunic pocket. Just as he started reading, Sarah Jane Smith, the journalist girl, walked in. Corporal Bryson leapt to his feet.

"Where's the Brigadier?"

"Out on the manhunt, miss, looking for the Doctor."

She screwed up her face. "What on Earth are you talking about?"

"Haven't you heard? The Doctor was the monster-maker. They caught him in the act but he escaped. Want a cup of tea?" The corporal had been feeling lonely, and liked the looks of Sarah.

"That's idiotic. What about Sergeant Benton and Captain Yates?"

"They're all out, too," said the corporal, "chasing after the Doctor."

"Then I'll go to General Finch's Headquarters. I'll leave a note for the Brigadier. Have you got anything I can write with?"

The corporal opened the Brigadier's desk drawer, and found some paper and a pencil. "Will this do?"

"Thanks." She sat down, and started writing.

"It wouldn't take a moment to make us both a cup of tea," said the corporal, hopefully.

"You're very kind," she said, still writing, "but there isn't a moment to spare—"

She stopped speaking as General Finch entered the classroom. If he was surprised to see Sarah he concealed it very well. "Where's the prisoner?" he asked Corporal Bryson.

"The prisoner, sir?" The corporal stood rigidly to attention. "He escaped, sir."

"I know that, man. He's since been recaptured. I just heard it on the R/T in my car. I presumed he'd been brought back here."

"No, sir. Not here, sir."

"In any case," interrupted Sarah, "the Doctor isn't

109

behind it all. I know who is. I was captured and escaped. I know everything."

The General stood with his feet apart, hands behind his back, and tapped his left calf with his swagger cane. "Do you, indeed?" He turned sharply to the corporal. "Dismissed!"

"Sir?"

"Get out!"

"Yes, sir!" Corporal Bryson saluted and hurried out of the classroom.

The General looked back toward Sarah. "You were saying, Miss Smith?"

Briefly, Sarah told General Finch what had happened to her. "And you know what I found when I opened that hatch? Steps leading down into a corridor in that underground control center!"

"What an extraordinary experience. But how did you get out of this place underground?"

She eagerly told him everything. "I snooped about for a while. Sir Charles Grover was down there having a chat with Professor Whitaker—"

The General cut in. "Is that the scientist you said had disappeared?"

She nodded. "I knew him from photographs I'd seen in the newspaper files. Anyway, they didn't see me. Eventually I found the elevator that Sir Charles Grover took me down in."

"I think your story deserves my personal investigation. Have you told it to anyone else?"

"There was no one here to tell."

"We must go to Sir Charles's office immediately. I think he has a lot to answer for."

Fifteen minutes later, the General's staff car drew up outside the deserted ministry. He and Sarah raced through the corridors then made their way upstairs to

110

the Minister's private office. It was empty. Sarah opened the door to the filing room which she knew to be a elevator.

"We go in here," she said. "And we press that button on the wall."

The General placed his finger on the button. The metal door slid across the carved wooden door and they heard the faint humming sound that Grover had said was the air-conditioning.

"We're really in an elevator," Sarah informed him. "It's very ingenious."

"Thank you," said General Finch. "You see, I devised it." He drew his Service revolver from its holster and aimed it at Sarah. "I'm sorry, Miss Smith, but you're a prisoner again."

She gasped. "I really do pick my friends."

"Perhaps we are more friendly than you imagine." He smiled, not unkindly she thought.

Nothing more was said until the General and Sarah had reached the main control room. Sir Charles Grover and Professor Whitaker looked up in astonishment.

"One Space traveler safely returned," said the General, slipping his revolver back into its holster. "Fortunately she's not spoken to anyone. Do, please, try not to let her escape again." He turned on his heel and went back down the corridor.

Grover laughed. "You're an intrepid young lady, Miss Smith! Well, what are we going to do with you now?"

"Well, you needn't put me back on that stupid spaceship. It's all a fake. What you're doing to those people is cruel. They all believe they're traveling to a new world."

"And so they are," said Grover. "But their new world—New Earth, as they call it—will be this one swept clean and returned to its early innocence."

111

Sarah tried to understand. "You're going to send them back into the past?"

"No, my dear. That, we have discovered, is technically impossible. Instead, Professor Whitaker is going to bring the past to them."

Professor Whitaker smiled. He always liked to hear his name mentioned. "I shall roll back Time to the Golden Age of youth, beauty, and innocence."

"Sarah asked. "And what about all the people alive on Earth now?"

"They'll know nothing about it," Grover answered her.

She tried to work it out. "Is that why you produced the monsters—to get people out of the way so they wouldn't be affected?"

"Why not tell her the truth?" said Whitaker. "She's going to realize sooner or later."

"It may be difficult for you to understand," Grover turned to Sarah. "When the Timescoop activates Operation Golden Age, the only people to remain in existence will be those in its immediate proximity. That is to say, the people in the spaceship and ourselves. The others will vanish."

"That's mass murder!"

"As I said," Grover continued calmly, "they will know nothing about it. We had to clear London so that undesirable people, people not approved by us as rightthinking, wouldn't be taken back through Time with us."

"What a disgusting idea," she blurted out, "to destroy the whole world because it isn't quite as you like it!"

"Eventually, you will see our point of view, Miss Smith." Grover straightened up. "Now we have much work to do. Operation Golden Age is close at hand. Professor Whitaker is about to materialize dinosaurs throughout London, finally, to clear the streets of soldiers, looters, and anyone else who may still be in the area. Then you will accompany us back through Time to the pure unpolluted world which we seek. The world as you know it will no longer exist, *and will never have existed!*"

9

Operation Golden Age

". . . Patrol 29 to Base. Time 0925 hrs. Monster sighted in Cornwall Gardens, Kensington. Believed to be tyrannosaurus rex. Am engaging with mortars . . ."

". . . Time 0927. UNIT patrol 57 to UNIT Headquarters. Pterodactyl at Tower of London is attacking the ravens. UNIT personnel moving in to fight and destroy . . ."

". . . Command to all Army and UNIT personnel in the Greater London Area. Tall fair-haired man—known as the Doctor, and proved responsible for monster invasion—to be taken dead or alive. Last seen near Marble Arch in stolen Army jeep. Repeat: to be taken dead or alive. By order of General Finch . . ."

". . . Finchley Road, North West London. Patrol 69 to base. Large monster, believed to be diplodocus, trapped in Alyth Gardens. Twitch of tail demolished synogogue and five houses. We are attacking with CS gas. Time 0945 hours . . ."

". . . General Finch to all patrols. Do not waste time seeking and attacking monsters during this new outbreak. Give top priority to apprehending the Doctor, who must be taken dead or alive. I repeat, concentrate on finding the Doctor. By order of General Finch, Commander-in-Chief, Greater London Emergency Area . . ."

114

The Doctor's stolen jeep screamed to a stop as a tyrannosaurus rex reared up in front of him. The Doctor put the vehicle into reverse gear, did a smart three-point turn, and drove off in the opposite direction—to find himself facing another tyrannosaurus rex. He swerved, crashing the jeep into the wall of a factory. Steam billowed from under the hood. The Doctor tried to start the engine again but even the self-starter wouldn't turn. Hearing the roars of the two monsters close behind him, he turned, expecting to have to duck from the open jaws. But the great reptiles were fighting each other, one tearing savagely at the other's neck. The Doctor seized his opportunity. He jumped out of the wrecked jeep and ran down the street. A small two-legged dinosaur, no taller than a dog, suddenly materialized beside him, snapping at his trouser legs. The Doctor kicked it away. It sprawled in the road, wimpering like a puppy.

The Doctor turned a corner. He had to find another vehicle. He must reach the control center and somehow destroy it. An army jeep was now approaching. Hoping to win over the soldiers, the Doctor raised his arms, motioning the jeep to stop. He put his best smile on.

The jeep stopped some yards away. A soldier jumped up from the back seat and carefully aimed a rifle at the Doctor's head.

"Don't shoot," called the Doctor. "I'm the one person who can help you!"

General Finch rose up from the seat beside the soldier. He pushed the soldier's rifle away. "Leave him to me!" he barked. He drew his revolver from its holster, released the safety catch, and took careful aim.

A voice from behind the Doctor shouted, "My prisoner, if you don't mind, General."

The Doctor swung round. The Brigadier had pulled up behind him in his UNIT jeep.

"Get out of the way, Brigadier," roared the General.

The Brigadier's voice remained calm. "I'm sorry, sir, but this man is a UNIT prisoner. I'm taking him into custody."

"I told you to get out of my way, Brigadier!" shouted the General.

The Brigadier turned to Sergeant Benton who sat in the jeep beside him. "Sergeant!" he ordered. Benton knew exactly what to do. Benton stood up and trained a sub-machine gun on the General.

The General's face turned scarlet. "You realize this is mutiny?"

"There's no question of mutiny," shouted the Brigadier. "I'm only doing my job."

For seconds they remained stock still, the General aiming his revolver at the Doctor, and Sergeant Benton training his sub-machine gun on the General and his soldiers. Then the General slipped back the safety catch, and returned his revolver to its holster. With as much dignity as he could muster he barked, "Brigadier, you will place this man under close arrest? I am holding you personally responsible for him." He sat down and nodded to his driver. With a look of relief on his face, the driver slipped the jeep into gear and drove away as fast as possible.

"Well, Doctor," said the Brigadier, "are you coming with us?"

"To be held in custody again, while these people destroy everything?"

"First let's go back to my Headquarters," said the Brigadier, "then we'll talk about it."

Professor Whitaker stepped back from the Time-scoop. "That's all I can do now until the power builds up again," he informed Sir Charles Grover and Captain Yates. "I've produced as many monsters as I can, certainly enough to finally clear Central London."

Yates turned to Grover. "What do we intend to do about Miss Smith, sir?"

"She won't be harmed in any way," smiled Grover. "I have great admiration for her spirit. That's why I tried to establish her on the spaceship. Sheer bad luck that she recovered consciousness too soon."

The military phone rang and Whitaker answered. "It's for you," he told Grover. "The General."

Grover took the phone. "Hello?"

"Finch here. The Brigadier's recaptured the Doctor. They held a gun on me, defied my orders. There was nothing I could do."

Grover didn't like that development, but was not a man for recriminations. "It doesn't matter now. We're into the final stage of Operation Golden Age."

"It jolly well does matter," replied the General urgently. "The Doctor has too great an influence on the Brigadier. What do you suggest we do?"

"I think it's best if you leave this to me now. You order the final evacuation of London—we want all these soldiers out of the way. I shall deal with the Doctor from my end."

He put down the phone before Finch could reply, and turned to Captain Yates. "Captain, there's something that only you can do. I hope that I can trust you completely . . ."

Butler led Sarah down a corridor and unlocked the door to a store room. It contained a number of empty tea chests and packing cases.

"Go in. You won't be in here long."

She looked around the little room, then back at Butler. "You'd be quite handsome without that scar, you know."

Over the years Butler had learnt to live with his disfigurement. He had got used to people looking away, pretending not to see it. "I can't help the way I look."

"Oh yes, you can. Plastic surgery would fix that. But there won't be any medicine or operating theatres back in this stupid Golden Age you people dream about. Still, maybe you like being ugly. It makes you look more sinister and criminal. How did you get it—in a fight?"

"Not exactly. I was a London fireman. I tried to save a child that had crawled out of an open window and was stranded on a high ledge. I managed to pass it to safety all right—but I fell thirty feet through a glass roof." He started to close the door.

"Please don't go," she called. "I said a terrible thing. I'm sorry!"

But the door closed and she heard the lock turn in it. She tried rattling the door handle, but the door was heavy and wouldn't budge. Then she caught sight of a small airvent high in the ceiling. She started to pile packing cases, one on top of another.

Corporal Bryson was removing the rest of the flags from the map of London. As he was taking down the map itself, the Brigadier, the Doctor and Sergeant Benton entered.

"What the blazes are you doing?" asked the Brigadier.

"Orders, sir," Bryson sprang to attention. "General Finch has issued a general order for all Army and UNIT personnel to leave London. I thought you'd know about it, sir."

"This is ridiculous," said the Brigadier. "The whole of London is crawling with monsters. What about the spotting patrols?"

"All gone, sir. Everybody is out of the zone."

The Doctor spoke up angrily. "Now do you see?

118

General Finch is just as involved as Sir Charles Grover, I'm pretty sure Captain Yates is in it, too."

The Brigadier slumped down at his desk. "Now that's one thing I cannot believe, not Mike Yates . . ." He caught sight of Sarah's note. He read it quickly and handed it to the Doctor.

"This confirms everything," said the Doctor. "The existence of the underground control center and Grover's involvement."

"But where the blazes is Sarah?" The Brigadier turned to Corporal Bryson. "When was this note left?"

"Very early this morning, sir. She went off with General Finch."

The Doctor and the Brigadier looked at each other. "There's no doubt about it," said the Doctor. "General Finch is in this up to the hilt of his ceremonial sword."

"Benton," snapped the Brigadier, "get me UNIT Headquarters in Geneva!" Although UNIT was in part under the jurisdiction of the British Army, the Brigadier's final authority was vested in the Supreme Headquarters of the United Nations Intelligence Taskforce at Geneva, Switzerland. The Brigadier turned back to the Doctor. "I shall speak to Geneva, and they can talk to the British Government in exile in Harrogate. The Government here will listen to Geneva, whereas I doubt if they'll listen to me."

"There's no time left for talking. We must attack that underground control center now," said the Doctor.

"Permission to speak," said Corporal Bryson, who was still standing to attention.

"What is it?" asked the Brigadier.

"Well, sir, are we evacuating or not, sir? I mean, should I remove all our things from this classroom?"

"Definitely not!"

"In that case, sir, what should I do?"

The Doctor gave the willing corporal a friendly smile. "Why not make us all a nice cup of tea?"

"Yes, sir!" The corporal grinned and hurried out of the classroom, happy to feel useful.

Sergeant Benton called to the Brigadier from his position at the radio transmitter apparatus in the corner. "I have Geneva on the line, sir."

The Brigadier reached for his desk phone. At the same moment Captain Yates entered from the corridor where he had been listening. "Cancel that call please, Sergeant Benton. We won't be needing it."

The Brigadier looked up. "Mike, what d'you think you're doing?"

The Captain pulled his revolver from its holster. "I'm sorry, sir. Please don't touch that phone. Doctor—Sergeant Benton—come and stand over with the Brigadier."

"Are you going to shoot us all, Mike?" asked the Doctor.

"Not unless you force me to. Sergeant, I told you to come and stand over here, otherwise I may have to kill the Brigadier."

Sergeant Benton slowly rose from his seat at the R/T apparatus and crossed the classroom.

"Captain Yates," said the Brigadier, squaring his shoulders, "I trust you realize how serious it is to hold a gun on a superior officer?"

Yates nodded. "I realize everything, sir. But our plan must go ahead."

The Doctor's voice was friendly. "How did you get involved in this, Mike?"

"It was after that business with the giant maggots in Wales. You remember I was sent on leave for quite a time."

"You were very disturbed," said the Brigadier. "I think you still are!"

120

The Doctor frowned at the Brigadier, as though asking him to keep his mouth shut. "Do go on, Mike."

"I had a lot of time on my hands, and I went along to one of the Save Planet Earth meetings and heard Sir Charles Grover speak. It convinced me."

"What do you hope to gain out of this?" asked the Brigadier. "To become Commander-in-Chief of their army or something?"

"I look for no personal gain, sir. All I want is a new world. Earth used to be a simpler, cleaner place. It has all become too complicated and corrupt. We intend to roll back Time."

"Can Whitaker really do that?" asked the Doctor.

"I believe so. All the preliminary experiments have been successful." Yates smiled. "We shall find ourselves in the Golden Age."

"Mike, believe me," the Doctor implored, "there never was a Golden Age. It's a myth, an illusion."

"Not this time," replied Yates. "We're going to make it all come true."

The Brigadier tapped his forehead. "I think you've gone potty, Captain. You're out of your mind!"

"I don't think there's anything wrong with Mike's mind, Brigadier," said the Doctor. "In fact, I sympathize with him in many ways." He turned to Yates. "But this isn't the way to change things, Mike. You have no right to obliterate the existence of generations of people."

"There's no alternative," said the Captain.

"Yes there is," replied the Doctor. "You can try to make something better of the world you've got. You humans can end the arms race, you can treat people with different colored skins as equals, you can stop exploiting and cheating each other, and you can start using Earth's resources in a rational and sensible way!"

Corporal Bryson entered the classroom carrying a

tray of tea mugs. "I didn't know you were back, Captain Yates. Care for a cup of tea, sir?"

Without thinking, the corporal had walked straight in front of Captain Yates's revolver. He stared at the muzzle pointing at his stomach, and in fright dropped the tea tray. Sergeant Benton leapt at the Captain, knocking the gun from his hand, while the Doctor's fingers slipped round the Captain's throat in a Venusian karate hold. Captain Yates went unconscious instantly and the Doctor gently lowered him to the floor.

"Sorry for interrupting, sir," said Corporal Bryson, overcome with embarrassment at having just smashed four Army mugs of tea. "I didn't realize what I was doing."

"You did very well," said the Brigadier. "You've probably just saved the world from extinction."

10

The Final Countdown

Mark and Adam helped the young woman down from the suspended-animation trolley. She was about twenty-five and dressed im the same style of blue denim as themselves. She swayed to and fro on unsteady legs once her feet had reached the ground.

"Welcome to the people," said Adam. "Who are you?"

The young woman blinked and looked about herself. "We're really on the spaceship?" She could remember nothing since she had sat in a chair and colored lights had blinked on and off, hypnotizing her.

"Indeed we are," said Adam, "and about to arrive on New Earth. Some of your friends have already recovered from the long period of suspended animation. Look." He indicated five other people, men and women, all in blue tunics. They were sitting about the main area of the spaceship, recovering from their long sleep. "What is your name?"

"Polly," she said, "Polly Anderson. Can we see New Earth yet?"

"If you go to that porthole," Adam pointed to one of the forward ports, "you can just see it as a disc in the depths of Space. It gets larger every day."

The young woman staggered away from them toward the porthole. Ruth entered from one of the corridors, a worried look on her intelligent face. "That girl's got out of the Reminder Room," she said.

"Really?" said Adam. "Well, she can't have gone far. Would you like to welcome our friends who have just revived?".

Ruth shot a glance at the group. "I'll speak to them later. You and I must search the ship for that girl. There's no knowing what she'll get up to. Come!"

Ruth swept out of the living area followed by Adam. Mark walked across to Polly Anderson who was having difficulty standing, and caught her arm. "Sit down and rest for a while. You'll soon feel better."

Out of the corner of his eye he saw Sarah signaling to him from the flight deck. Quickly glancing round to make sure no one was watching, Mark hurried across to the flight deck's glass door and opened it.

"I just got back," panted Sarah. "That door"—she indicated the hatch that supposedly opened into Space—"it leads you straight into the corridor of a control center under London."

"I don't believe it."

"Then how do you think I'm alive?" She went to the hatch and yanked back the lever. Mark peered out and saw a flight of wooden steps leading down into a corridor. "Do you believe me now?"

He looked away. Sarah saw that his eyes were glistening with tears. "I honestly believed we were traveling to a new world," he said simply. "We've all been tricked." He sniffed. "But why? What are the organizers doing this for?"

"It's very complicated," she explained. "We've got to explain to the others." She flung open the glass door, and went into the main living area. "I want everyone to listen to me," she announced, raising her voice. "This is all a trick. You're not on a spaceship, and you're not going to another planet."

124

The people who had just revived from suspended animation turned to look at Sarah in dazed disbelief. The young woman whom Mark and Adam had just revived didn't understand at all. "I'm Polly Anderson," she smiled. "Who are you?"

"It doesn't matter who I am," said Sarah. "Please will you all pay attention to me. It's a big trick. We are on Earth. This spaceship is a fake."

A middle-aged balding man was the first to grasp what she was saying. "I find that difficult to believe. They made promises to us. I went into everything very carefully. I resigned my position as bank manager and even sold my house!"

"I'm afraid she is telling the truth," said Mark.

Ruth and Adam entered. They stopped in their tracks when they saw Sarah. "How did you escape from the Reminder Room?" Ruth demanded.

"It doesn't matter. I'm trying to tell everyone you've all been tricked. I've escaped from this so-called spaceship, and returned. We are deep under Central London. It's all fake. I'm going to prove it to you all by opening the hatch inside the flight deck."

Sarah turned to go back into the flight deck. Ruth grabbed her arm. "This poor girl is unbalanced. She should never have been selected. She's already contaminated one of our number." She pointed an accusing finger at Mark.

"Let me go," shouted Sarah. "I want to prove that you're wrong!"

"Never! Someone help me hold her. If she opens that hatch we'll all be killed. You, girl, give me a hand!"

Polly Anderson obeyed the command by grabbing Sarah's other arm. "I thought everything was going to be peaceful," she said, "not all this sort of thing."

"Two of you grab the boy," Ruth commanded.

125

"They must be restrained until we have safely landed."

The ex-bank manager and another man pinioned Mark's arms behind his back. "Where to?" asked the ex-bank manager.

"Follow me," said Ruth, and with Polly's help marched Sarah down the corridor leading to the Reminder Room.

Adam entered into the flight deck and studied the communications system. He pressed a button marked "TRANSMIT," and spoke into a microphone. Would anyone hear him across the reaches of Space? "Hello? Hello? Can anyone hear me?"

Adam's voice came clearly through a loudspeaker set in the wall close by the Timescoop. Sir Charles immediately strode up to the communications console. "How do I make this thing give static?"

Butler hastened to Grover's side and adjusted some knobs. "This will make it sound as though you are talking by radio across Space."

Grover spoke into a microphone that had the words SPACESHIP written above it. "This is spaceship number one. We are receiving you loud and clear."

Adam's voice came through the loudspeaker. "I must speak to Charles Grover. Something very strange has happened here. The girl Sarah claims we are not on a spaceship."

Grover shot a glance at Butler, then spoke into the microphone again. "This is Charles Grover speaking. Where is the girl?"

"We have just locked her in the Reminder Room."

Butler listened for a moment, raced away toward the storeroom in which he had locked Sarah. Grover spoke authoritatively into the microphone. "Please take no hasty action on your ship. As you know, I can reach you by shuttle in a few minutes. Over and out."

126

Whitaker looked up from the Timescoop. "Well that's a fine kettle of fish, I must say!"

"Where's the space-walking gear?" asked Grover.

Whitaker pointed to the cupboard. "All in there. It's a good thing we thought of that."

Grover opened the cupboard. Inside hung a replica of an astronaut's space-walk suit. He began to put it on.

Butler ran breathless into the room. "She's gone! Went through the airvent. She'll tell them everything."

Grover was pulling on the heavy trousers over his expensive suit. "Twenty years in politics has taught me that people only believe what they want to believe." He paused to think. "I suppose that goes for us all in a way."

A giant stegosaurus was standing peacefully outside Westminster Underground Station contemplating the Houses of Parliament. It thought that the great gray buildings were other monsters; if it stayed very still perhaps they would leave it alone. Then a small and very mobile monster came hurtling around the corner making a lot of noise and smell. It stopped with a screech. An even smaller creature jumped out of it and threw something. There was a loud bang and a flash of fire that disturbed the stegosaurus's peace of mind.

"It's doing you no harm, Brigadier," shouted the Doctor. "Leave the poor thing alone."

The Brigadier, about to hurl another hand grenade, paused. "All right. Let's go into the station."

They grabbed their supply of dynamite, and hurried into the station and down the steps.

"I never thought I'd find myself blowing up a London underground station," said the Brigadier. "If you're wrong, Doctor, I'm going to have a difficult job explaining all this to London Transport."

❉ ❉ ❉

". . . The conveyor-belt system of mass production brings drudgery to the workers. Their natural creative drive is stifled. They are slaves to the machines. Working in continuous noise, unable to speak to their fellow workers, they are brutalized . . ."

Sarah put her hands over her ears. "Can't we turn that film off?"

Mark shouted above the sound of the running commentary which filled the Reminder Room. "It comes on automatically whenever the door is closed and someone is in here."

Suddenly it stopped and the door opened. Sir Charles Grover, dressed in his spaceman's suit and carrying a heavy helmet, stepped into the room. He left the door slightly ajar for fear of restarting the film.

"You really are a terrible problem to me, Miss Smith," he said.

She looked at him in astonishment. "Why are you dressed up like that?"

Grover lowered his voice confidentially. "You and I know this is a fake spaceship, but the people outside still believe in it. So I had to pretend to arrive by shuttle and come through the airlock. They think I've been space-walking."

Mark's anger burst. "You've cheated us! Why didn't you tell us all the truth in the first place?"

"He didn't dare tell you," said Sarah heatedly. "Don't you understand, Mark? Millions of people are going to be wiped out." She swung round to Grover. "That's true, isn't it?"

He nodded slowly. "I'm afraid it is. But it will be quite painless. They will never have existed. You see, I had to tell a story that would be acceptable to good people like Adam and Ruth and Mark, the kind of people that I wanted to recruit."

Sarah said, "You mean decent people who might object to the destruction of generations of other human beings?"

"I am only deceiving them about the means, not the end. They will have their New Earth, but it will be this Earth returned to an earlier, happier time."

"The end can never justify the means," protested Mark. "You've implicated us all in a terrible crime against humanity!"

Grover appealed to Mark. "Will you, for the sake of the others, accept the situation?"

"No. Never!"

"Then my only hope," confessed Grover, as he moved back to the door, "is that once this great project is complete, you will adjust to life in the Golden Age. I'm deeply sorry about this. I hope that in time to come we will be friends again." He closed the door. Almost at once moving pictures of squalid overcrowded blocks of flats appeared on the screen.

". . . the brutalization of millions of people extends from the factories to the buildings in which they live. To accommodate an ever increasing population vast tenement blocks are thrown up in our cities, providing no sense of community for the unfortunates who dwell in them. Gone is the concept of the village . . ."

Sarah banged on the door. "Mark, we've got to get out of here!"

"I don't think there's an escape route."

Sarah looked around desperately: there was no airvent in here, nothing. "I think you're right." She leant against the wall in exhaustion. "Do you know, I think I'm going to cry."

"If you do," he said, "try my shoulder. It's broad enough."

"Thanks. I may take you up on that—"

The door opened and Adam slipped in quietly from the corridor. "Are you two all right?"

129

"We're O.K.," said Mark, thankful that the film and its running commentary had stopped when the door opened. "But you've got to help us."

"I know. You see, I listened at the door when Grover was talking to you. Do you realize the man is a raving lunatic?"

"I don't think he is," said Sarah. "He knows exactly what he's doing."

"Maybe." Adam tugged thoughtfully at his beard. "The question is—what do *we* do?"

"Stride into the flight deck," said Sarah, "open that hatch and show everybody the truth."

Adam said, "Ruth won't like that."

"People like Ruth never do like the truth, but this time she's got to face up to it. Now let's go and open that hatch."

Adam and Mark followed Sarah out of the Reminder Room.

On the platform at Westminster Underground Station the Doctor and the Brigadier were poised to blast their way into the elevator shaft that led to the control center. Using a battery-driven drill, the Doctor bored holes into the floor of the broom cupboard.

"You're absolutely sure," asked the Brigadier, who was preparing the sticks of dynamite to go into the holes, "that this is the right broom cupboard?"

"No doubt about it," said the Doctor. "They've concreted the floor. Once we blast that away, we shall be into the elevator shaft."

A sudden roar abruptly stopped their conversation. The Brigadier swung his torch round. Filling one end of the tubular platform area was a triceratops—nine tons of horned dinosaur with a mouth like a beak.

"Good grief," exclaimed the Brigadier, "that must be the ugliest one of the lot!"

The Doctor turned around to look. "The neck-frilled variety," he commented. "They used to roam in great herds across North America, and could charge up to thirty miles an hour, impaling their prey on those horns."

"Most interesting," said the Brigadier sarcastically. "But what's it doing down here?"

"They must know we're trying to break in, so they've materialized that to distract us." The Doctor started drilling again and shouted over the noise. "It's stupid really, because charging animals are always at a disadvantage in a confined place."

"Perhaps it doesn't know it's at a disadvantage, Doctor," replied the Brigadier, "because it's coming toward us."

"Keep it away somehow," said the Doctor, concentrating on his work.

"Certainly," said the Brigadier. "I'll go and say 'boo' to it." He desperately scrabbled in the bag of equipment he had brought down from the jeep. To his delight he found a set of flares for use as distress signals. He picked one up, lit it, and walked a few feet toward the triceratops. The monster opened its beaked mouth in fury, roared, and backed up the platform.

"I think you've *all* three gone mad," said Ruth, as she faced Adam, Mark and Sarah in the main living area of the spaceship.

"You could at least listen to us," Adam pleaded.

The ex-bank manager stepped forward. "That sounds reasonable enough—to listen."

"All right," Ruth said, "what have you to tell me?" She sounded just like a headmistress addressing naughty children.

"It's perhaps best if you watch." Sarah crossed to the

flight deck and opened the glass door. "I'm going to open that hatch."

"You'll only kill yourself," said Ruth, "and kill us at the same time."

"No, I'll close this glass door first. Then I'll only kill myself. Now watch!"

Sarah closed the glass door. The whole group, including the reluctant Ruth, moved to the door to watch. Sarah went up to the hatch and yanked the lever. The door opened. Sarah stood at the open doorway and breathed in and out, letting them see her chest rise and fall.

Adam turned to Ruth. "Are you convinced now?"

Ruth pulled open the glass door. "Where do you say that door leads to, girl?"

"To the people who have cheated you. I'll show you the way."

"All set," shouted the Doctor. He had just finished attaching terminals to the sticks of dynamite set in the floor of the broom cupboard.

"Just as well," said the Brigadier. "I'm running out of flares."

The Doctor ran along the platform toward the steps, uncoiling wire all the way. The Brigadier threw his final flare at the monster and then followed him. Halfway up the steps the Doctor stopped. He attached the wires to a detonator. "Here goes, Brigadier!" He rammed down the plunger. From the platform they heard a huge explosion.

"Where's the rope ladder?"

"Here." The Brigadier searched in his bag of equipment again, and produced a very fine nylon rope ladder. "I'll go down there with you."

The Doctor shook his head. "Less chance of being spotted if I'm alone. You go and summon up some reinforcements. See you soon, I hope." He hurried away into the cloud of black smoke which still billowed from the center of the explosion, while the Brigadier went up the stairs to get to his jeep and radio in for troops to be sent if any were still in the London area.

The Brigadier's voice came over Sergeant Benton's earphones. "Brigadier Lethbridge-Stewart to UNIT Headquarters. We need troops urgently at Westminster Underground Station."

"Yes, sir," Benton replied into the microphone. "I can contact one mobile patrol. It's all that's left in London."

"Good man. Send them here as fast as possible. Over and out."

General Finch stood by Benton, his service revolver pointed at the sergeant's neck. "You will forget that request for troops, Sergeant."

"But sir, if the Brigadier's in danger . . ."

"The Brigadier is clearly aiding and assisting an escaped detainee. He will be court martialed, and so will you if you act on his instructions."

The sergeant hung his head, signifying compliance with his superior officer's orders. "Very good, sir. Just as you say, sir."

The General smiled and lowered his gun. "I'm glad you see it my way, Sergeant—"

Benton suddenly leapt to his feet. As his clenched fist swung into the General's jaw bone, he said, "Very sorry to have to do this, sir."

The General saw the fist too late. It crashed into his jaw bone, stunning him instantly. He fell heavily to the floor, his revolver spinning away from his hand.

Sergeant Benton grabbed his sub-machine gun and helmet and hurried out of the classroom.

Professor Whitaker looked up from the controls of the Timescoop. "Everything's ready."

Grover looked worried. "General Finch should be here."

"I hope you don't propose to wait. The timing is crucial."

"He must be in the area," said Butler. "As long as he's inside the protective field, he'll be scooped up with us."

"That's true," agreed Grover, and turned to Whitaker. "All right, Professor Whitaker. Let us now return to the Golden Age."

Whitaker put his hand on the lever that would activate the Timescoop and roll back Time. "Just think of it, a moment from now I shall have achieved what everyone believed to be impossible."

"Indeed so," said Grover, glancing at his watch. "Would you like to get on with it?"

"You just don't want me to have my moment of glory, do you?" Whitaker pouted. "All right, I'll pull the lever."

"Stop! We shall have no part of this!"

The trio standing by the Timescoop swung round to see Adam entering the control room. He was followed by Ruth, Mark, Sarah, and a group of people dressed in blue denim tunics. Grover was the first to recover from the shock. He shouted at Whitaker. "Go ahead! Do it *now!*"

The bank manager and Mark pushed past Grover and pulled Whitaker away from the controls.

"You've cheated us," Ruth accused. "We know all about you."

Grover looked at the people who were now menacing him. "My dear friends, I haven't cheated anyone. Let me pull that lever and you will have the Golden Age that I promised you."

"You're going to destroy all the civilizations of Humankind," said Adam. "All the great literature of the ages, every work of art—everything will vanish. Leaving Earth for another planet was one thing, but this is evil."

"Civilization has already destroyed Humanity," Grover replied. "It's time to make a fresh start. If we take the Earth back in Time, we can guide Humanity along a better path. Just think of it—we can give it a second chance!"

The bank manager moved away from the Timescoop. "That's true, you know. Do we really want to keep the world as it is?"

Grover was grateful for an ally. "Now is our chance to build the world anew. Are we to let that opportunity slip through our fingers?"

"He's right," said Ruth. "And why should we lose our chance of personal happiness? This is what we all planned. I say that we complete the plan!"

"No," protested Mark, "it's criminal!" He turned to face Ruth. "The only reason you want to go ahead now is because you can't stand being made a fool of! You must never be wrong!" He turned to the remainder of the group. "If we allow that lever to be pulled we shall become as evil and self-seeking as the things we hate in this present world!"

"Quite right," said the Doctor as he entered from the corridor that led to the elevator shaft. His clothes were dusty after his climb down the rope ladder. "None of you will be fit to enter your so-called Golden Age if this is the means you intend to use to get there."

"Congratulations, Doctor," said Grover. "You are in time to be present at the most important moment in the world's history."

"On the contrary," said the Doctor." I am in time to

135

prevent a crime." He looked over his shoulder. "And fortunately I am not alone."

The Brigadier, Sergeant Benton, and half a dozen UNIT soldiers entered from the corridor, all as dusty as the Doctor from their climb down the elevator shaft.

"No one is to move," ordered the Brigadier. He pointed across the control room at Professor Whitaker. "Kindly stand away from those controls."

Grover turned quickly to Whitaker. "Go ahead. *Now!*"

Whitaker pushed Mark aside, and leapt for the lever that would activate Operation Golden Age. His hands grasped it firmly, and he pulled downward with all his might.

Slowly the Brigadier, Benton, and the UNIT soldiers began to walk backward into the corridor. Adam, Ruth, Mark, Sarah, and the group from the spaceship went through all their most recent actions in slow-motion reverse, and then started to move backward out of the control room.

Being a Time Lord, the reversal of Time did not completely affect the Doctor. As though swimming through a sea of oil, the Doctor forced himself forward toward the lever of the Timescoop. As his hand reached out to touch it, he saw that Professor Whitaker and Grover—who stood nearest to the Timescoop—were already dematerializing. The Time eddy swirled all around the Doctor, its great force seeking to drive him back into the corridor from which he had come, but he struggled forward. His fingers reached the lever, touched it, curled round it. Exerting himself to the utmost, he pushed the lever slowly back into position.

Instantly Time moved forward again. The group from the spaceship trooped back into the control room, followed by the Brigadier and Sergeant Benton and the UNIT soldiers.

136

"No one is to move," commanded the Brigadier. He looked across to where Professor Whitaker had been standing. "Kindly stand away from those controls . . ." His voice trailed off. He turned to the Doctor. "Where's Whitaker?"

"I imagine he and Sir Charles Grover have returned to their Golden Age," replied the Doctor. "Perhaps they will be happier there."

The Doctor started up the jeep which he had borrowed from the Brigadier, and drove Sarah away from Westminster Underground Station. Slowly, thoughtfully, he turned it into a deserted Whitehall. It was not until they neared Trafalgar Square that either of them spoke.

"If Sir Charles Grover and Professor Whitaker really traveled back in Time," said Sarah, "it means they were in our past. But that's impossible."

"Is it? Why?"

"Well, we'd have heard of them."

"Surely that depends at what point in the past they arrived." The Doctor turned the jeep into Charing Cross Road. A flock of pigeons, unaccustomed to traffic for the past fortnight, flew up from the road as the vehicle approached.

"It would have changed our history," continued Sarah.

"Not if they were already there."

She ran her hands through her hair. The bump was going down. "I find it very confusing."

"Only because you think of Time as one continuous process. But what if Time goes backward and forward, or round in big circles?"

"If people from the future turned up in the past," she said, emphatically, "we'd know about it!"

"Perhaps we do." The Doctor drove the jeep slowly

round Cambridge Circus. "You know, there's a book you might try reading sometime."

"What's that?"

The Doctor stopped the jeep and looked up and down Charing Cross Road, London's center of bookshops. "Well, let's see what we can find." He drove on a little further and stopped the jeep outside Foyle's. The front doors had been battered in by the swish of a monster's tail. "We might find it in here."

He strode into the deserted bookshop. Sarah followed him, calling. "We could be shot as looters!"

"We're not going to take anything," said the Doctor, "just browse a little. Ah!" He saw a sign reading RELIGIOUS DEPARTMENT and went toward it. By the time Sarah caught up, the Doctor was looking into a copy of *The Holy Bible*.

"Read that," he said, pointing to a page. "It's Ezekiel, Chapter 1 verse 5–6."

Sarah read: "Also out of the midst thereof came the likeness of four living creatures. And this was their appearance; they had the likeness of a man. And every one had four faces, and every one had four wings."

She looked up at the Doctor. "Who were these creatures?"

The Doctor shrugged. "Perhaps they were from another planet, or from the future of this planet." He replaced the book on its shelf.

They got back into the jeep and turned north toward UNIT's temporary Headquarters. "There are so many mysteries," said the Doctor as they headed up the Tottenham Court Road. "Remember what I told you about the *Marie Celeste*? The whole Universe is full of mysteries. The important thing is to keep an open mind."

SPECIAL PREVIEW

DOCTOR WHO #4
AND THE GENESIS OF THE DALEKS

Terrance Dicks

It was a battlefield.

The ground was churned, scarred, ravaged. Nothing grew there, nothing lived. The twisted, rusting wrecks of innumerable war machines littered the landscape. There were strands of ragged, tangled wire, collapsed dugouts, caved-in trenches. The perpetual twilight was made darker by fog. Thick, dank and evil, it swirled close to the muddy ground, hiding some of the horrors from view.

Something stirred in the mud. A goggled, helmeted head peered over a ridge, surveyed the shattered landscape. A hand beckoned, and more shapes rose and shambled forward. There were about a dozen of them, battle-weary men in ragged uniforms, their weapons a strange mixture of old and new, their faces hidden by gas masks. A star shell burst over their heads, bathing them for a moment in its sickly green light before it sputtered into darkness. The *thump* of artillery came from somewhere in the distance, with the hysterical chatter of automatic weapons. But the firing was some distance away. Too tired even to react, the patrol shambled on its way.

A man materialized out of the fog and stood looking in bewilderment after the soldiers. He was a very tall man, dressed in comfortable, old tweed trousers and a loosely hanging jacket. An amazingly long scarf was wound round his neck, a battered, broad-rimmed hat was jammed onto a tangle of curly brown hair. Hands deep in his pockets, he pivoted slowly on his heels, turning in a complete circle to survey the desolate landscape.

He shook his head, the bright blue eyes clouded with puzzlement. This was all wrong, he thought. It was all terribly wrong. The transmat beam should have taken him back to the space station. Instead he was here, in this terrible place. How could it possibly have happened?

"Greetings, Doctor."

The Doctor spun around at the sound of the voice behind him. A tall, distinguished figure in flowing robes stood looking at him quizzically. A Time Lord! The Doctor knew all about Time Lords—he was one himself. He had left his own people untold years ago to roam through Space and Time in his "borrowed" TARDIS. He'd rebelled against the Time Lords, been captured and exiled by them, and had at last made his peace with them. He had served them often, sometimes willingly, sometimes not. These days their hold on him was tenuous. But it was still a hold, a limitation of his freedom, and the Doctor never failed to resent it.

He glared at the elegant figure before him. "So! I've been hijacked!" he said indignantly.